FREDDY THE PIED PIPER

"There, you see?" he said. "Two cents—that's his price."

FREDDY
the
PIED PIPER

by WALTER R. BROOKS

Illustrated by Kurt Wiese

THE OVERLOOK PRESS
WOODSTOCK & NEW YORK

If you enjoyed this book, very likely you will be interested not only in the other Freddy books published in this series, but also in joining the *Friends of Freddy,* an organization of Freddy devotees.

We will be pleased to hear from any reader about our "Freddy" publishing program. You can easily contact us by logging on the either THE OVERLOOK PRESS website, or the Freddy website.

The website addresses are as follows:
THE OVERLOOK PRESS:
www.overlookpress.com

FREDDY:
www.friendsoffreddy.org

We look forward to hearing from you soon.

First published in the United States in 2002 by
The Overlook Press, Peter Mayer Publishers, Inc.
Woodstock & New York

WOODSTOCK:
One Overlook Drive
Woodstock, NY 12498
www.overlookpress.com
[for individual orders, bulk and special sales, contact our Woodstock office]

NEW YORK:
141 Wooster Street
New York, NY 10012

Dust jacket and endpaper artwork courtesy of the Lee Secrest collection and archive.

Cataloging-in-Publication Data is available from the Library of Congress

Brooks, Walter R., 1886-1958.
Freddy the Pied Piper / Walter R. Brooks ; illustrated by Kurt Wiese.
p. cm.
Summary: When the animals of Mr. Blooschmidt's traveling circus need help, Freddy the pig does not disappoint them.
[1. Pigs—Fiction. 2. Domestic animals—Fiction. 3. Circus animals—Fiction. 4. Circus—Fiction.] I. Title.
PZ7.B7994 Frl 2002 [Fic]—dc21 2001059344
Manufactured in the United States of America
ISBN 1-58567-226-2
1 3 5 7 9 8 6 4 2

Chapter 1

It had been a hard winter. A foot of snow had fallen on the 3rd of December and another foot on the 10th, and then the mercury crawled down to ten below and stayed there until after Christmas. Then it warmed up just enough to snow some more. And the weather kept on like that for another six weeks. It was still that way on the morning of February 14th, when Freddy, the pig, crawled out of his warm bed and went to his study window and looked out and said disgustedly: "Oh, my goodness sakes!"

The windowpanes were frosted up so that he

could only see out of the upper quarter of them, and they were made of old-fashioned glass that was so crinkly and full of bubbles that what he did see through them was so twisted and warped that it was hard to tell what it really was. Of course Freddy rather liked this. He said it made the things he saw twice as interesting as they really were. If, for instance, his friend Charles, the rooster, went by, his neck might be drawn out long, so that he looked like an ostrich, or his head might be completely disconnected from his body and float along above him. Whereas seen through a clear pane of glass he was just Charles, and nothing to think about much.

But today nobody was going by, and there was nothing to be seen but dazzling snow which stretched from the window sill in an unbroken sheet up to meet the blue sky. And Freddy had said: "Oh, my goodness sakes!" partly because he was sick of the snow, but more particularly because today was St. Valentine's Day, and he had hoped the mailman would bring him some valentines. But the mailman hadn't been up the road past the Bean farm in over a week, and he certainly wouldn't try to buck those drifts in his old Ford today, even to bring Freddy a valentine.

So Freddy sighed and was just turning back to crawl under the quilts again when he saw something moving. It was long and low and grey, and it might have been a shed, only there wasn't any shed down by the gate, and anyway sheds don't move around. Even though the glass made everything he saw through it look queer, Freddy usually could guess what things were if he wanted to, but he couldn't guess what this thing was. He took a rag and wiped a pane, but the rag wasn't very clean and just blurred it more than ever. And then the thing moved on out of sight of his window. "Oh, shucks!" said Freddy and went back to bed.

He shut his eyes and took up his dream again where he left off. It was a nice dream. He was opening stacks of valentines, and each valentine had a dollar bill in it. It was rather like Christmas, only better because there were no names signed to the valentines and so there wouldn't be any thank-you letters to write. But he had only opened about fifteen when there came a tap-tap-tap, and it woke him and he opened his eyes and there outside the window was Charles, tapping on the pane.

Freddy got up and went to the window rather grumpily, and put it up and let the rooster in.

"Morning, Freddy," said Charles. "There's a rhinoceros here to see you."

"There's a what?" said Freddy. "Oh, cut the funny stuff, Charles."

"Funny, nothing!" said Charles. "There's a rhinoceros. He wants to talk to you."

"Oh, yeah?" said Freddy. "I guess you aren't awake yet this morning. I guess you're still dreaming, and your dreams are just as impossible as mine are. I just dreamed that you gave me a dollar for Valentine's Day."

"Look, Freddy," said Charles; "I put myself to a good deal of inconvenience and discomfort to bring you this message. My feet are darn near frozen, and I fell through the crust three times between here and the barnyard. But if that's all the thanks I get . . . calling me a liar . . ."

Freddy said: "Hold on! Hold on! If you say it's a rhinoceros, O K—then it's a rhinoceros. But I still think . . . Well, the only rhinoceros I ever knew was the one that was in Mr. Boomschmidt's circus, and he's down in Virginia with Mr. Boomschmidt."

"Sure—that's the one," said Charles. "He's come all the way up here to see you. Came on foot every inch of the way, too, and he's got an awful cold."

"I should think he would have," said Freddy. "Coming up north in the winter time. What does he want?"

"Why don't you go down to the cow barn and find out? You're the one he asked for."

It would have been a lot easier to stay in the warm pig pen and make guesses as to what the visitor wanted, than to go down in the cold and find out. But though rhinoceroses are pretty tough animals, they are not accustomed to a cold climate, and Freddy realized that this one would not have taken such a trip unless his errand was important. So he started for the cow barn.

Like all lazy people, Freddy was capable of doing long stretches of really hard work. He was lazy in streaks. He was lazy about things he wasn't interested in, but there were a lot of things he was very much interested in, and in his short life he had accomplished more than many children of the same age. But he often spent more time and energy in getting out of a job than it would have taken to do the job in the first place.

One of the things he didn't like was shoveling snow. Mr. Bean had kept the paths around the barnyard open all winter, but the path to the pig pen was Freddy's job. He could either keep that path shoveled out, and be free to come and go, and to see his friends, and get his three meals a day, or he could let it go and hibernate all winter like a woodchuck in his hole.

Well, of course he tried to have it both ways. In December, when the snow was a foot deep, he didn't bother to shovel because he could wade through it all right. When it got to be two feet in January he still didn't shovel it, because he could still flounder back and forth through it. But when it got to be three feet deep and over his head, he had to do something. So he took his shovel and he opened his door and looked at the snow piled against it higher than his head, and then he shut the door again and leaned the shovel in the corner, and sat down in his big chair and thought.

The result of his thinking was that he decided to drive a tunnel down to the barnyard. That would be no more work than shoveling, and a lot more fun. More practical, too. For it would be warmer in the tunnel than outdoors, and if it blew he would be out of the wind, and if it snowed he wouldn't get all wet and chilly. And it wasn't like shoveling: if he did it once he wouldn't have to do it again. So he opened the door and went to work.

Well, of course, before he had driven his tunnel three yards the whole thing caved in on him, and he almost smothered before he got back to the door again.

But even then he didn't start shoveling. Because he had an old pair of skis in his study, and he said: "It will certainly take me less time to learn to ski than to shovel out the path, and then I can go on top of the snow. That will be even more fun than a tunnel, because not only can I whiz down to the barnyard in about three seconds, but I can ski all over the farm, and even down to Centerboro to the movies if I want to."

Well, the skis were better than the tunnel, but he didn't whiz down to the barnyard in any three seconds. The first time it took him two hours, and the second time he lost one ski, and a rescue party headed by Mrs. Wiggins, the cow, had to come out for him. But after that he got so that he could manage the skis pretty well. Though his friend Jinx, the cat, figured out that in the time he had lost and wasted he could have shoveled a path through the snow six feet deep and three miles long. Of course, I don't know if his figures were right. But Freddy didn't care anyway. He hadn't done any shoveling.

All winter it had been cold and the snow had

packed hard and dry. But the night before the rhinoceros came it had warmed up and rained a little, and then it had frozen, so that there was a crust over the snow that was as slippery as glass. Freddy didn't realize this. He put on his skis and stepped out on the snow. And it was a good thing that the skis were pointed towards the barnyard or goodness knows where he would have ended up. For the minute the skis touched the icy crust, they started. Freddy gave a yell of surprise and pushed backwards with the ski poles to keep from falling, and then the whole farm seemed to come whizzing up towards him, and past him, and though it was a still day the wind whistled in his ears; and then before he knew what had happened the dark square of the cow barn door rushed at him and swallowed him, and there was a crash and a thump and he was sitting on a hard floor with a pain in his shoulder and a lot of comets and constellations whirling around his head. And when these cleared away he couldn't see anything.

Through the darkness came Mrs. Wiggins' voice. "Goodness, Freddy! Are you all right?"

"I'm blind!" said Freddy. "Oh dear, I'm blind! I can't see you or anything."

"You've got your eyes shut," said Mrs. Wiggins.

"Why—that's right!" Freddy opened his eyes. He was sitting on the floor, and the three cows were standing over him, watching him with anxious concern. "I'm all right," he said. "That is—I guess I am. Wrenched my shoulder a little." He got up and shook himself, and then he laughed. "Bet I did it in three seconds that time all right!" he said.

"There's somebody here to see you, Freddy," Mrs. Wiggins said.

"Oh, yes, the rhinoceros," said Freddy. "Where is he?"

"We put him over in the box stall in the stable," said the cow. "He's got a bad cold, and we thought he'd be more comfortable there. Mr. Bean has been looking after him."

So Freddy limped over to the stable. He found the rhinoceros lying in the corner on a pile of hay with a blanket around his shoulders. He looked pretty miserable, but rhinoceroses always look miserable, even when they're in the best of spirits.

"Hello, Freddy," he said. "My, I'm glad to see you! I had quite a time finding your place.

I must say these Beans you live with are nice people. Soon as I got here and they saw I had a cold they hustled me right in here where it's warm, and covered me up with a blanket, and Mrs. Bean made me a pailful of hot lemonade. I'll be fit as a fiddle by morning."

"Well, it's nice to see you, Jerry," Freddy said. "I don't suppose you made the trip for pleasure, though. Is there anything wrong with Mr. Boomschmidt?"

Jerry shook his head sadly. "There ain't much that's right, Freddy. You see, he hasn't been able to take his circus out on the road for four years, because war conditions made traveling out of the question. That wouldn't have been so bad, because he's got that place down south and we thought we could all live there until he could start out again. He had quite a little money put by, and he figured out a regular budget—so much for coal, and so much for electricity, and entertainment, and all the things you spend money on; and it worked out that we could all stay there and have a good time and not do a tap of work for five or six years.

"Well, it worked out nice on paper, but when we came to the end of the first year—well, Freddy, the money was all gone."

"Gone! You mean it was stolen?" Freddy asked.

"No. It was all used up. Mr. Boomschmidt hadn't figured it right. In making out this budget thing he hadn't put anything down for food. And food for lions and tigers and giraffes and . . . why, do you know how much hay one elephant eats at a meal?"

"No," said Freddy. "How much?"

"I don't know, but it's an awful lot. And then when meat was rationed, the lions and tigers had to go on a vegetable diet. You ought to have seen Leo making faces over his supper—a big bowl of oatmeal."

Leo, the lion, was an old friend of Freddy's, and had often visited at the Bean farm. "Where is Leo?" Freddy asked.

Jerry shook his head. "I don't know. When Mr. Boomschmidt couldn't afford to feed us any more, he sent around to different zoos to see if they'd take some of us. They took the giraffe and two of the elephants and some of the smaller animals. But they wouldn't take lions and tigers because they couldn't get meat for them. So finally Mr. Boomschmidt called us all together and he said: 'Boys, you know how things are. If any one of you has got a plan, well my goodness, let's hear it!' Of course nobody had any plan. 'Well then,' he said, 'the only thing for us to do is to scatter and live off the country. If we stay here, we'll starve. Of course,'' he said, ''if I could find Col. Yancey's treasure, we'd all be fixed. But we haven't had much luck with that.' ''

''What's the treasure?'' Freddy asked.

''Oh, there's supposed to be some money hidden in the old house. At least folks around there say this old Col. Yancey that used to own the place hid it before he went off to join the Confederate army. Mr. Boomschmidt has hunted for it some, but it's been more a game than anything else: he doesn't really believe it's there.

'' 'Well,' he said, 'how about it? There's lots of wild country around here and, my goodness, your forefathers managed all right, in the days before there were any circuses. Eh, Leo—didn't they manage all right?' You know how the chief always wanted Leo to back him up.

''Well, Leo backed him up all right, though I guess he didn't know much about how his forefathers managed, seeing he wasn't there. But he said the chief was perfectly right and it was the only thing to do, and the other animals agreed. So we decided not to put it off, but to start right away. Leo made a little speech and thanked Mr.

Boomschmidt for all he'd done for us, and then we said goodbye." The rhinoceros sniffed damply, and wiped his eyes with the corner of the blanket. "It was pretty sad, Freddy. I don't like to think about it. Mr. Boomschmidt and his old mother, and Madame Delphine—you remember, she was the fortune teller with the circus—they stood there in the porch and watched us marching off to the woods. Tears running down their faces.—Tears running down our faces too, of course." Jerry sniffed again. "Got a handkerchief? Oh, never mind; here's some Kleenex Mrs. Bean brought me."

Freddy was very much affected by the rhinoceros' tears. Mr. Boomschmidt and his animals were old and valued friends, and this account of their misfortunes made him sad. But Freddy was practical in such matters and he didn't think that he and Jerry would help Mr. Boomschmidt much by crying on each other's shoulders. Besides, having an animal who weighs nearly a ton crying on your shoulder is no treat. So to keep Jerry from breaking down completely he said gruffly: "Snap out of it, Jerry. I'll do anything I can for Mr. Boomschmidt, but you haven't told me yet what you want me to do."

Jerry wiped his eyes on half a box of Kleenex, sneezed twice, and then said: "You're right, Freddy. Well, there isn't much more to tell. It was last spring—nearly a year ago—that we took to the woods and separated, and what has become of the rest of the animals I don't know. I struck out northwest, into the mountains. Had a real nice summer, too. I kept to the hills, and I don't suppose any of the farmers or village people in the valleys ever guessed there was a rhinoceros living close by.

"But one day last fall I was lying up in a blackberry patch—you never saw such berries, Freddy; they were as big as plums—well, small plums, anyway . . . I was on the edge of the woods above a valley, and I saw what I thought was a big yellow dog running across the fields below me. You know I don't see very well; I have to rely on my ears and my nose; but the wind was from me to him so I couldn't tell much about him. But all at once he stopped, and then came bounding up towards me, and I knew he'd scented me."

"And it was Leo, I bet," Freddy put in.

"Darn it, Freddy, you spoiled my story," said Jerry peevishly. "Oh yes, it was Leo. Just as I started to charge him, he roared. I'd know that

The rhinoceros sniffed damply, and wiped his eyes with the corner of the blanket.

roar anywhere. Well, we were pretty glad to see each other. But Leo was awful thin. He said: 'You know, Jerry, this wild free life isn't all it's cracked up to be. All I've had to eat in the last two weeks is a couple of owls and a woodchuck. And that's pretty poor pickings.' And then he said he'd decided to strike north and try to reach here. ' 'Tisn't only on my own account, Jerry,' he said. 'We ought to do something to help the chief. He's been good to us for a long time, and now when he's in trouble, what are we doing to help him? Walked out—that's what we did, just walked out.'

"I said I didn't see what else we could have done, and he said no, he didn't either, but he said when Mr. Boomschmidt was in trouble there was no excuse for our not doing everything we could. 'And I figure it,' he said, 'that Freddy and the Bean animals—they're good friends of the chief's—they'll maybe be able to think of something.'

"Well, that's the story, Freddy," Jerry said. "We decided to try to reach you, and see if you and your friends could think up some way of helping to get the chief back into the circus business. We don't want you to *do* anything, Freddy; we just want an *idea*."

Chapter 2

Of course Freddy was greatly flattered to be so highly thought of. If Jerry had walked all the way up from Virginia to get his advice, then his advice must be pretty valuable. And he at once put on a very solemn and important expression and said: "H'm! Ha! Yes, quite so"—all of which was intended to show Jerry that he had come to the right place if he was looking for wisdom. But Jerry just peered at him with deep concern and said: "What's the matter—you got a stomach-ache?"

"Certainly not," Freddy said crossly. "I'm thinking."

"Gosh!" said Jerry sympathetically. He never did much thinking himself, and he evidently felt that it was a pretty painful process. As of course it is.

He didn't say anything more and continued to look earnestly at Freddy, blinking his weak little eyes, as if expecting the idea he had asked for to pop out any minute. And when he had waited quite a while and nothing had happened, he said: "Aren't you going to help me, Freddy? Leo said you were just full of ideas."

"I am," said Freddy. "Of course I am. The trouble is I've got so many that it's hard to select just the right one for the job. I'll have to think this over for a while. You stay covered up, Jerry. I'll be back soon."

Freddy knew it was no use trying to get back to the pig pen over that icy crust, so he went into the next stall where Hank, the old white horse, lived. Hank had overheard the conversation and he said: "Land sakes, Freddy, that's too bad about old Boomschmidt. If he was in trouble, why didn't he send word to us?"

"I suppose he hated to ask for help. Felt

ashamed, I expect, because he couldn't support his animals any more."

"Don't see how it was his fault," said Hank.

"It wasn't. But what I don't see is, why Leo hasn't managed to get up here. Of course he couldn't have come along the main roads, because he'd have been seen, and maybe shot or captured. But Mr. Boomschmidt lives in Virginia, and that isn't so far but what he could have worked up through the back country in all this time."

"Well, I don't suppose it's as easy as it looks," said Hank. "Nothin' ever is. Exceptin' maybe slidin' down hill on skis," he added with a snicker.

"I don't suppose I'll ever hear the last of that," said Freddy resignedly. "There's one thing about the animals on this farm—they hang on to a joke the way old Zenas Witherspoon hangs on to an old hat, until it's so smashed and stained and full of holes that if it wasn't on his head you wouldn't know what it was. Why, there are some jokes around this farm that were here before I was born, and I don't believe anybody but maybe Mr. Bean knows what they mean any more."

"They must be pretty good jokes, then," said Hank, "to last all that time. And I don't know, Freddy—there ain't anything like a good old time-tested joke, that you don't have to stop to think whether it's funny or not; you can just go ahead and laugh your head off.

"Well, I think—" Freddy began, and then he said: "Hey, listen!" There was a deep humming sound that grew gradually louder, and they ran to the door and saw the snow plow coming slowly up the road. The animals all went out and shouted and waved to the men on the plow, and then somebody said: "Here comes the mailman!" and sure enough, way down the hill in the direction of Centerboro they saw a black speck coming up the white groove that the plow had cut through the snow.

There was quite a stack of letters. Freddy got six, and there were several for Mrs. Wiggins, and all the animals—even the mice—had one or two. There was a big white envelope for Mrs. Bean, and the animals called her to the back door and stood around while she opened it. It was a beautiful lacy valentine all decorated with hearts and arrows and clasped hands, and on it was this verse:

I love my pipe
And my tobaccy;
I love you,
I do, by cracky!

I can't write pretty
For I ain't a poet,
But I love you,
And don't I know it!

If you ditched me
I sure would pine,
So I hope you'll be
My valentine!

"My land!" said Mrs. Bean, and she giggled and blushed, and then she turned to Mr. Bean, who had come to the door behind her. "So that's the way you spend your time when you ought to be splitting me some firewood!"

"Pshaw!" said Mr. Bean, looking embarrassed. "Don't know what you're talking about, Mrs. B." And he puffed so hard on his pipe that both of them disappeared in a cloud of smoke.

The animals began opening their valentines. The two ducks, Alice and Emma, had one addressed to both of them. It read:

Oh, Emma, Alice, Alice, Emma,
I'm in a terrible dilemma.

You're both so fair, I can't decide
Which one I'd like to make my bride.

I cannot think which one I'd druther,
For each is lovelier than the other.

So Alice, Emma, Emma, Alice,
I pray you do not bear me malice,

But share this poor devoted heart,
Cut right in two by Cupid's dart.

They quacked excitedly over it. "Oh, sister, what a lovely valentine!" Emma exclaimed. "I wonder who could have sent it!"

"Whoever it is," said Bill, the goat, "he isn't taking any chances. The guy ought to make up his mind."

"I expect it's that brown duck over at Witherspoons'," said Georgie, the little brown dog. "I've seen him wandering around on the edge of the woods above the duck pond a number of times. I expect he's too bashful to come down and call."

"If there's one thing I can't abide," said Mrs. Wiggins, the cow, "it's a bashful duck. Bashfulness is bad enough in other animals, but a duck looks so silly shuffling his feet and rolling his eyes and peeking out from behind things."

"I don't agree with you, dear Mrs. Wiggins," said Emma. "Most of the young people today are so bold and forward—it is very refreshing to find one who doesn't feel so sure of himself."

"He isn't young," said Georgie. "He's quite a middle-aged duck."

"Sillier than ever," said Mrs. Wiggins, but Alice and Emma didn't agree; they felt that his bashfulness was merely a sign that he had been well brought up; and when the other animals realized that they were really much interested in this mysterious suitor they didn't say any more.

Freddy had opened his valentines. They were mostly jokes and verses from other animals on the farm. He could guess pretty well who had sent them. Perhaps the nicest was a very pretty one which had a five dollar bill pinned to it. It was from Mrs. Winfield Church, a rich friend of Freddy's, who lived in Centerboro. She was a very generous woman and always sent the animals presents on Christmas and on their birthdays, but Freddy was her special favorite because he had helped her out several times when she had been in difficulties, and almost every holiday she sent him something. Usually it was money, because she said: "It's hard to know just what to give a pig. But money is always useful." This had been going on for some time, and Freddy was by now a pretty well-to-do animal.

Among the valentines was even one for Jerry. It read:

Here's to you, Jerry; we all join together
  In welcoming you to our home.
You came all this way in the worst kind of
    weather,
  For it couldn't be colder in Nome.

You had no red flannels to keep yourself warm
  And you had no galoshes or hat,
But you plugged right along in the teeth of the
    storm,
  And we surely admire you for that.

So you're here, and we're glad, and we all want
    to say,
  Though of valentines we've quite a few,
The best of the valentines we'll get today
  Is from our friend Boomschmidt—it's YOU!

Jerry read it, and then he said: "Well!" And then he read it again and said: "Well . . . my goodness!" And then he sniffed damply and blew his nose several times, though whether it was tears coming to his eyes or just his cold, nobody could tell. Rhinoceroses aren't usually very emotional.

Freddy's mind was pretty well occupied with Mr. Boomschmidt and his troubles, and he wanted to talk them over with his friend Jinx. But the cat wasn't around.

Mrs. Wiggins laughed. "Oh, that Jinx!" she said. "He's so wrapped up in what he calls 'his art' that he's hardly stuck his nose outdoors in two weeks. He's probably up in his studio."

So Freddy went back into the stable and climbed the steep stairs into the loft where Mr. Bean's Uncle Ben had once had his workshop. Jinx had set up an easel there and had cleared a space on the workbench for his paints and brushes, and around the walls were hung the pictures he had painted. Most of them were portraits of Jinx himself—sitting up, lying down, crouched ready to pounce—but all looking very handsome and intelligent and at least twice life size. On the easel was a half-finished picture of

Jinx, and beside it stood a mirror in front of which lay the cat, apparently asleep.

"Hi, Jinx!" Freddy shouted. And as the cat gave a start and opened his eyes, he said: "Asleep, hey? So that's what you do up here."

"I was not!" Jinx said crossly. "I was looking in the glass—painting my picture."

"Oh, sure," said Freddy. "Painting with your eyes shut."

"Of course I had my eyes shut," said the cat. "That's the way they are to be in the picture. It's a picture of me asleep."

"You can't ever see what you look like asleep," Freddy said, "any more than you can see between your shoulder blades."

"I can see between my shoulder blades," said the cat, and he twisted his head around to show the pig.

"Oh, all right," Freddy said. "Look, Jinx. You can't see yourself in the glass unless your eyes are open. So if you want to paint your picture with your eyes shut—"

"I shut 'em, and then I open 'em very quick," Jinx said. "I open 'em just before my reflection opens 'em, so that just for a second my reflection has his eyes shut and I can see what it looks like. See?"

"Hi, Jinx!" Freddy shouted.

"No," said Freddy, "but it doesn't make any difference." He looked around. "You must be awful stuck on yourself to paint nothing but your own portrait all the time."

" 'Tisn't that, Freddy," Jinx said. "There isn't anything else to paint. None of you other animals will pose for me. Hank gets cramps in his legs, and Mrs. Wiggins goes to sleep, and—"

"You could paint landscapes," Freddy said.

"What landscapes? Look out that window and show me a landscape I could paint."

Freddy looked. It was true there was very little to see. Just the broad expanse of white, broken only by the line of a fence and a tree trunk or two. Then he looked around at the one or two little landscapes Jinx had done last fall before the snow came, when he first started painting. Each of them had a little label under it—"Woodland Peace," or "Giants of the Forest," or "Moon Shadows." This last showed the pigpen in the foreground, and Freddy grinned. "Very fanciful titles," he said. "When the moon comes over the pigpen—we could make a song of it. But I don't agree with you that there's nothing to paint. Do a snow scene." He propped up a blank canvas board on the easel, then with a brush made two horizontal lines for the fence and above them, two thicker vertical lines for the tree trunks. "There you are," he said. "There's your landscape. Slap in a little blue sky above it and you've got 'Winter Fields' or something, and my goodness, you can paint twenty of them in an hour and not use up more than a couple squeezes of paint."

"Golly, I believe you've got something there," said Jinx. He backed off and squinted at the picture with his head on one side. "Yes, sir, that's art with a capital A."

"Pooh," said Freddy. "That's nothing. But look here, Jinx. I need your help." And he told him about Mr. Boomschmidt.

Jinx was interested at once. He tossed aside his palette and brushes and sat down and listened intently, and then he scratched his head. He didn't scratch it as you or I would scratch our heads—he scratched it with his left hind foot, but it meant the same thing—that he was thinking deeply. And at last he said: "I'm afraid you've tackled a job that's too big even for you, Freddy. To get even a little one-horse circus like Mr. Boomschmidt's on the road again would take a lot more money than we could ever raise. Money to hire the clowns and the bareback riders and the men to put up the tents and look after the animals, and more money to buy the food for them all. And if you did all that, you still wouldn't have the animals. According to Jerry, they're scattered all over the country by this time."

"Maybe so," Freddy said. "But I've got to try. Mr. Boomschmidt is my friend, and so are Leo and the others. But of course if you don't want to help—"

"Who said I didn't?" Jinx demanded. "We've always tackled things together, haven't we? I'm with you from whiskers to tail, Freddy." He knocked his unfinished portrait into a corner. "Kind of sick of looking at my own face in a mirror for weeks on end, to tell you the truth."

"I didn't suppose you ever got sick of that," said Freddy with a grin. For Jinx was proud of his good looks.

But the cat shook his head. "To be quite frank with you, Freddy, I didn't suppose so either. Shucks, everybody likes to—well, let's be honest —everybody likes to admire himself. You do it, I do it, everybody does it. It's animal nature. But I don't know." He looked at his friend with a puzzled frown. "It's all right for a while. You keep finding new things that you like—the way your eyes sparkle, or how noble you look when you hold your head back a little. But pretty soon you begin to notice other things. Maybe it's a little squint in one eye, or a kind of foolish expression when you smile. And you sort of begin to wonder . . ." He stopped and shook his head again. "It don't do to study anything too long, even your own face," he said. Then he shook himself and said: "Well, what do we do first?"

"The first thing," said Freddy, "is to go down to Centerboro. I've got a sort of plan, and we'll see if it works."

Chapter 3

Half an hour later Freddy and Jinx set out on the long walk to Centerboro. Freddy hadn't been able to get back to the pigpen, and he bundled up in an old shawl that he borrowed from Mrs. Bean. As he trudged down the long groove made by the snow plow with Jinx at his side, he looked like a little old woman out for a walk with her pet cat. Jinx of course had a warm coat of his own fur and didn't need anything else.

When they reached Centerboro they went

right to the bank, and Freddy asked for the president, Mr. Weezer. As the founder and president of the first animal bank in the country, Freddy was well known in banking circles, and they were shown at once into Mr. Weezer's office.

The banker greeted them cordially, shook hands with Jinx, and then leaning back in his chair tapped the side of his sharp nose with his glasses and said: "And now, gentlemen, what can I do for you?"

So Freddy told him about Mr. Boomschmidt. "And we'd like your advice, sir, as to what we can do to help him get his circus started again."

"H'm," said Mr. Weezer. "Ha. I know Boomschmidt. A fine man. But it takes a lot of money to get a circus going. Even if he had all his animals."

"A thousand dollars?" Freddy asked.

"More than that. Well, perhaps if he was willing to start small, a thousand would do it."

"Would your bank lend him a thousand dollars?" Freddy asked.

Mr. Weezer shook his head. "Couldn't do it. If it was my money, I might take a chance. Boomschmidt's a good fellow, and I'd like to help him. But the money we have in this bank isn't mine; it belongs to the people who have left it here for safe keeping. So when I lend any it has to be on good security."

"What's security?" Jinx asked.

"Oh, you know, Jinx," Freddy said. "When you borrowed twenty-five cents from the First Animal Bank to buy that catnip mouse, you had to leave your best collar with the bank. Then if you couldn't pay the twenty-five cents back, the bank could sell the collar and get its money. You put up the collar as security."

"That's it exactly," said Mr. Weezer. "If Mr. Boomschmidt has any good security to put up—"

"How about Jerry?" said Jinx, and Freddy said: "Oh, sure. Mr. Weezer, how much would you lend on a rhinoceros in good condition?"

"A rhinoceros? Why, we lend money on animals sometimes—cows and horses and pigs—excuse me, Freddy. But if Mr. Boomschmidt couldn't pay up, what would the bank do with a rhinoceros?"

"You could sell him."

"Who to? Barclay," he said to a small man in a green eyeshade who came in at that moment, "what are rhinoceroses quoted at today? Will you look it up, please?"

The man looked surprised. "Rhinoceroses, sir? Never seen any quotations on them. Pigs are firm today, sir. Chickens are off two cents, and lambs very weak. But rhinoceroses—not a very active market in them, I should say." He paused a moment, then laid a sheaf of papers in front of Mr. Weezer. "I thought you ought to see these, sir," he said. "Just brought them up from the vault."

Mr. Weezer put on his glasses and examined the papers, the edges of which seemed to be badly chewed and tattered. "Tut, tut!" he said. "Worse and worse!" He held them out to Freddy. "Mice," he said. "Chewing up half the important papers in our vault. I wish I knew how they get in. Of course it's an old vault, and there are cracks here and there. They ate up a whole package of five dollar bills two nights ago, and now here—here's two war bonds half eaten and Jacob Wensley's note—they've eaten the corner where the amount was written, and now we won't be able to collect. Don't know how much he borrowed now. I don't suppose you remember, Barclay?"

Mr. Barclay thought it was either a hundred and fifty or seven hundred, he couldn't remember which.

"There you are," said Mr. Weezer. "Of course Jake has lost all his money and can't pay

anyway, but it's the principle of the thing." He
looked at Jinx. "You wouldn't want a good
mouse-catching job around here for a few weeks,
would you?"

"I'm sorry," Jinx said. "I don't catch mice any
more—haven't in years. Why, some of my best
friends are mice."

"We've been trying to borrow a cat," said Mr.
Weezer, "but it's a big year for mice, and everybody that has a cat wants to keep it to protect his
own property. Well, it's too bad; if you could
have helped me out, I might have done something for Boomschmidt."

"I might be able to help," said the cat. "I
know about mice. They don't tear papers up
just to be mean. It's usually to make nests, unless
they're terrible hungry, and then I guess they'd
eat them. Why don't you strew a lot of old newspapers around in the vault?"

"You think they'd chew them up instead?"

"I've got an idea," said Freddy. He drew up
to Mr. Weezer's desk and took a sheet of paper
and a pencil and began lettering a sign. It read:

ATTENTION MICE!!

These newspapers are provided by the man-
agement for your convenience. Use them free-

ly, but please do not disturb any other papers. Free cheese will be distributed every Thursday as long as you comply with this request.

by Henry Weezer, *President.*

Mr. Weezer read it, said: "Good!" and passed it to Mr. Barclay. "See that this is taken care of at once," he said. "And while you're at it go out and buy a couple pounds of cheese."

Mr. Barclay hesitated. "That'll look sort of funny on the quarterly statement," he said. "Under 'Expenses'—two pounds of cheese."

"Nobody ever reads our quarterly statement anyway," said Mr. Weezer. "But I'll explain it to the Board at our next meeting." And then when Mr. Barclay had gone he thanked the two animals warmly. "You come and see me again in three or four days," he said. "If this works, maybe I can figure out something that will help Mr. Boomschmidt more than lending him a few dollars on an old rhinoceros."

From the bank, the two animals walked over to the jail. The prisoners were having a snowball fight in the jail yard. They were all bundled up warm except the sheriff, who was refereeing. He was dressed as he always was, winter and summer, in his shirtsleeves, with his silver star pinned on his vest. When he saw Freddy he left the game and went over and invited the animals into his office.

"Glad you came," he said. "I was getting pretty chilly." He shivered and broke a small icicle off the end of his moustache. "Pull chairs up to the stove and tell us the news."

"I should think you'd be frozen," said Freddy. "Why don't you wear a coat?"

"Well, I tell you," said the sheriff. "Folks in this town expect their sheriff to be a pretty tough character. If they thought I was a sissy they wouldn't vote for me. But when they see me out there in the cold in my shirtsleeves, they say: 'My land, our sheriff's a pretty tough customer! He's the kind of man we want.' And next election I get their votes. It's just politics." He shivered. "It ain't much fun and it don't make sense, but you got to give folks what they expect."

"Is that why you carry that pistol sticking out of your hip pocket?" Jinx asked.

The sheriff laughed. "I carried a pistol my first term in office," he said. "Though it wasn't ever loaded. But it was pretty heavy, so I sawed off the butt and had it just sewed into the pocket so it sticks out. Now when I get me a new pair of pants, I have 'em made complete with a pistol butt in the hip pocket."

"I know a way you could make people think you were even tougher," said Freddy. And when the sheriff appeared interested, he said: "Well, you know if anybody owns a big fierce dog, they always think he's a pretty tough man. Well, suppose you had a pet rhinoceros?"

"A pet rhinoceros, eh?" said the sheriff. "Why yes; yes, that would be—" He stopped suddenly. "Hey, what are you trying to put over on me?" He demanded. "You got a rhinoceros you're trying to get rid of or something?"

"We're not trying to put anything over," Freddy protested. "Wait, I'll tell you." And he told the sheriff about Jerry's visit, and Mr. Boomschmidt's trouble. "You see," he said, "we want to get the circus started again, and we want to keep Jerry until we do. But we can't ask Mr. Bean to feed him all the rest of the winter. He eats an awful lot of hay, and the hay crop wasn't very good last summer; Mr. Bean has only got about enough in the barn to take care of his own animals. I know you've got a lot of hay in the barn back of the jail that the prisoners cut last July—"

"That hay belongs to the county," said the sheriff. "I can't just use it to feed stray rhinoceroses. What would the taxpayers say?"

"I see," said Freddy. "Well, you feed the prisoners out of county money. Suppose the rhinoceros was a prisoner. Suppose you arrested him and put him in jail. You'd have to feed him then."

"What can I arrest him for?" the sheriff asked. "He ain't broke any laws. There ain't any law against being a rhinoceros. Though I don't know," he added thoughtfully, "when you look at one of the critters you wonder sometimes why there isn't."

"Couldn't you keep him as a sort of watchdog?" Jinx asked.

"Wait a minute," said the sheriff. "I got an idea. I'd like to help you boys out if I can, and I just thought: I'm allowed a certain amount of money for recreation and entertainment for the prisoners. Suppose I took him as a pet for the boys, eh? Is he broke to harness? Some of 'em's been after me to get 'em a pony—maybe this would do."

Freddy said: "He's not broken to harness. But he's goodnatured. He isn't very bright, though."

"Well, suppose you had a pet rhinoceros?"

"That would be all right," the sheriff said. "Most of the prisoners ain't any too bright, either. He'd fit right in. I wouldn't want to bring in an animal that was brighter than the prisoners are; they might think I was trying to teach 'em something, and prisoners and school kids are a lot alike: there ain't anything that makes 'em madder than to think you're trying to teach 'em something." He smiled at the two animals. "Well, that's settled. You bring Jerry down. I'll keep him for you for a while, anyway."

Chapter 4

Next day Freddy took Jerry down to the jail. The rhinoceros was feeling much better, and before they went Freddy had him plow out a path to the pigpen. He just took Jerry out into the barnyard and pointed him up the slope towards the pigpen and said: "Go!" and Jerry put his head down and shut his eyes and went. He went through the deep snow like a baby tank, and it was lucky that Freddy hadn't pointed him directly at the pigpen, but a little to one side, for

even if he'd had his eyes open, they were so weak
that he probably wouldn't have seen it, and if
he'd hit it he would have knocked it into smith-
ereens. Indeed, he went on quite a distance beyond it before he heard Freddy yelling to him to
stop. But now Freddy had his path open, and he
hadn't shoveled it himself either.

Freddy and Jinx spent the rest of the day trying to find out if any of the birds in the neighborhood had heard or seen anything of Leo. For
they were worried about the lion. He had started
north the same time Jerry had, "and he must
have got into trouble," Freddy said, "or he'd
have been here by this time." But the birds
hadn't heard anything—or rather, they had
heard too much. For the sky is always full of
gossip; everything that happens is seen and
noted by some bird or other, and is passed on
from beak to beak in the continual chatter of
the birds, so that if a boy gets spanked in Texas
it is known twenty-four hours later in Maine.
But the trouble is that the story changes a good
deal in the telling. Each bird adds a little as he
passes it on, just as people do when they repeat
a bit of gossip, so that after it has been repeated
half a dozen times it isn't very much like what
originally happened. And so Freddy and Jinx

got a lot of interesting stories about strange animals that had been seen here and there, but none of them sounded much like Leo.

"The only thing to do," said Freddy, "is to paint a picture of Leo and show it to the birds. You can do that, Jinx."

"I can't paint from memory," said the cat. "If you had Leo here, so he could pose for me—"

"Well, he isn't here," said Freddy. "Look, I'll pose for you—as Leo." He went up to the pigpen and found a wig of long yellow curls that he had used as one of his disguises when he was doing detective work, and a piece of rope with a frayed-out end. He put the wig on for a mane, and tied the rope on for a tail, and then he came down into Jinx's studio and stretched out in as lion-like a pose as he could assume, with his head held proudly high and a very noble and snooty expression on his usually kindly face. "How's that?" he said.

"You don't look much like a lion," said Jinx. "Golly, I don't know what you do look like!" Then he began to laugh. "Yes, I do, too. You look like a pig dressed up as a little girl. A nice little girl." And he laughed harder than ever.

"Oh, shut up!" said Freddy crossly. "Little girls don't have long tails."

"Lions don't have long snouts, either," said
Jinx. "Look, can't you sort of snarl?"

Freddy curled his lip up. It wasn't a very good
snarl. It just made him look sort of half-witted,
but the cat didn't want to make him mad, so he
said: "O K," and picked up his brush and went
to work. He didn't want to laugh any more, but
of course he had to keep looking at Freddy, and
every time he looked at him his whiskers
twitched and he sort of shook inside. Until at
last Freddy said: "What's the matter—are you
trying not to sneeze?"

"Nose itches," said Jinx, and he took a paint
rag and scrubbed his nose to hide the grin that
kept pulling the corners of his mouth up towards his ears. When he took the rag down he
had smeared yellow paint all over his nose, and
that made Freddy laugh, so then Jinx was able
to laugh too, and they both laughed hard for
quite a long time. And then Jinx went to work
with his brush and slapped on the yellow paint—
swish, swish, swish—with quick sweeps, and in a
very short time he had his picture finished. It
really did look a little like a lion.

They hung the picture up on the outside of
the cow barn and then invited all the birds to
come and look at it. Dozens came, and they chat-

Freddy curled his lip up.

tered and twittered and giggled and made bad
jokes about it the way birds do, but none of them
could say that they had seen any animal that
looked like that—indeed several of them said
they didn't believe there ever was such an animal. Freddy said: "I guess we'll have to wait till
the bluebirds and robins begin coming up from
the south next month. They're more likely to
have seen Leo than the birds that stay around
here all winter."

But at last three chickadees came; they were
from the southern part of the state and were vis-
iting friends in Centerboro, and their names
were Mr. and Mrs. Lemuel Spriggs and their
daughter, Deedee. And when Deedee saw the
picture she gave a weak little chirp and her eyes
turned up and she fell right off her branch into
the snow.

Mrs. Spriggs screamed and carried on like
everything, and Mr. Spriggs tried to quiet her,
but neither of them tried to help Deedee, and
it was Jinx who waded out into the snow and
picked her up in his mouth and carried her over
to the back porch. He miaouwed and Mrs. Bean
came and let him in, and he took the chickadee
and put her in the cigar box under the stove
where the mice slept. Mrs. Bean fed her milk

with a medicine dropper, and by and by Deedee opened her eyes and said weakly: "Where am I?"

Well, Deedee came around all right and pretty soon she was hopping about the kitchen floor and picking up some crumbs that were left over from dinner, and the four mice watched her sharply with their beady little black eyes because the crumbs really belonged to them, but they didn't like to say anything because she was a guest. Freddy tried to ask her what it was that had scared her so, but Mrs. Spriggs said: "Oh, no questions, please! The child has had a dreadful shock. She must have complete rest."

Freddy said: "Well," doubtfully, but Jinx said: "Nonsense! What scared you, Deedee?"

So then Deedee told them. She and some of her little friends had been playing tag around through the back yards of the town where they lived—it was a place called Tallmanville, in the southern part of the state. And they saw a piece of suet hanging outside a back window of one of the houses. Naturally they supposed it had been put there for them, since a good many people put out suet for birds in the wintertime, and they all gathered around and began pecking at it. And all of a sudden, out of the open window beside which it hung came a big paw which scooped up three of the chickadees and pulled them into the house. The others shrieked and flew off, but as she went, Deedee caught a glimpse of a large yellow animal which looked a good deal like this picture. That, said Deedee, was why the picture had scared her so.

"Why, Deedee," said Mrs. Spriggs, "you never told me about this!" And she began to scold her daughter.

"I was afraid you'd tell papa," said Deedee, "and he's so brave—he'd have gone around there to beat up that animal and maybe got caught too. I didn't want that."

"Child's making it all up," said Mr. Spriggs. "Really, Deedee, a big yellow animal! No animal ever looked like that picture."

"I'm not so sure," Freddy said. "Tell me, Deedee; do you know who lived in that house?"

Deedee said sure she did; it was a Mrs. Guffin; she kept a pet shop.

"I know the place," said Mr. Spriggs. "The front part of the house is the shop, with a show window with some dogs and cats and canaries in it." He laughed. "You saw Mrs. Guffin, Deedee. She's a big woman with yellow hair; looks a lot like this—what did you call him, Freddy—a lion?"

Freddy said: "Yes." He looked thoughtfully at Deedee. "I think your father's right, Deedee," he said. "It could hardly have been a lion that you saw."

"I should think not!" said Mrs. Spriggs crossly. "The child has just made the story up. She ought to be spanked."

But Freddy said he thought that Deedee had been honestly mistaken, and shouldn't be punished for that, and Mrs. Spriggs agreed with him; and they comforted Deedee, who had begun to cry because she thought she was going to get spanked, and gave her some bird seed from a can that Mrs. Bean kept handy for just such emergencies.

But when the Spriggs had gone, Freddy said: "I don't know. It's best to let them think that she really didn't see a lion, because we don't want a lot of talk. But suppose that was Leo she saw?"

"Yeah, I've been wondering about that," said Jinx.

"We'll just have to go down to that Tallmanville place and find out," Freddy said. "Maybe it isn't Leo but something's happened to him or he'd be here by this time. We can't take a chance. Why, he might be a prisoner in that house."

"Sure, sure," said Jinx. "But how are we going to get there? It's two hundred miles."

Freddy said: "We'll hitchhike. I'll wear one of my disguises—let's see, I guess that old dress and Mrs. Bean's big shawl over my head. I'll be a poor old Irishwoman. Nobody would refuse to give a poor old Irishwoman a lift."

It didn't sound very good to Jinx, setting out on such a trip in the dead of winter. But though, like most cats, he liked the comforts of home, he was a good deal of an adventurer, too, and—well, this trip looked as if it might turn into a first class adventure. So he just said: "O K. When do we start?"

They started early next morning, and sure enough, as Freddy had predicted, they had not trudged along more than half a mile through the snow before a truck came rumbling up behind them and stopped, and the driver said: "Want a lift?"

"Ah, the blessings of the saints on ye, kind man," said Freddy as he climbed in. "Would ye be drivin' south, now?"

"Only to Centerboro," said the man. "Is that your cat?"

"Sure and whose else would it be? Come, kitty; hop in, me little darlin'."

Jinx jumped in and sat on Freddy's lap and the truck went on.

"That's a fine cat," said the man. "Is he a good mouser?"

"Och, 'mouser' is it?" said Freddy. "Sure there's not a mouse within ten miles dares show a whisker inside my house. You'd not think he was so ferocious to look at him, would you now?"

"You can't tell to look at 'em," said the man.

"Ain't that the true word! Meek as Moses he looks, but a roarin' lion he is when wid mice!" Freddy gave Jinx an affectionate hug. "Ah, but it's a sweet ickle sing he is. He's his mama's ickle cutums, he is."

Jinx, who disliked being made fun of, and specially when he couldn't hit back, unsheathed his claws and dug them quietly into his friend's shoulder. Freddy started violently, but the man didn't notice.

"How far you going, ma'am?" he asked.

"To Tallmanville."

"That's a long ways," said the man, and he thought for a while and then said: "It's a terrible year for mice. I expect it's because there's so much snow they've all come indoors, and they're educated mice, too—they kick the traps over and spring them and then eat the bait. Last night

they ate all the soap out of the soap dishes. And
of course you can't get a cat anywheres. All the
kittens in the county are spoken for before they
get their eyes open. So I tell you what I'll do,
ma'am; I'll drive you right through to Tallmanville myself if you'll let me have the loan of that
cat. Just for a couple of weeks."

Well, it would have been an easy way to get
down to Tallmanville, but Freddy knew that
Jinx would never consent. So he said: "That's a
fine generous offer and sorry I am that I can't be
takin' it. For sure, what would I be doin' without pantry protection those two weeks? It's eatin'
me little house right out from under me the
mice would be."

The driver was a reasonable man and he
agreed that that was probably true. So he
dropped them on the outskirts of Centerboro,
where the road into the town crossed the main
road going south. Freddy thanked him, and they
went on southward. There weren't many cars on
the road, and they walked several miles before
one finally drove up behind them and stopped,
and a woman's voice said: "Want a lift?"

Freddy recognized that voice, and he recognized the hand, glittering and flashing with
many rings, that came out of the car window and

beckoned. It belonged to his old friend Mrs.
Winfield Church. He thought he would see if
he could fool Mrs. Church with his disguise, so
he pulled the shawl closer around his face and
when the chauffeur stepped out and opened the
door, he climbed in and said: "Oh, ma'am, sure
you're very kind to a poor old widow woman.
Hop in, kitty-my-love, and don't be messin' up
the beautiful upholstery with your great clumsy
wet paws."

"Not kind at all," said Mrs. Church. "Drive
on, Riley. I like company and Riley here has
been driving me for twenty years and we're
pretty well talked out. How far are you going?"

"To Tallmanville," said Freddy, "to visit me
married daughter."

"Why, we go through Tallmanville, don't
we, Riley?" said Mrs. Church.

"We *can,*" said the chauffeur over his shoulder. "But it's out of our way." He glanced
around. "What part of Ireland are you from,
ma'am?" he asked.

"From Ballyhooblin, in County Mayo," said
Freddy quickly.

"Aha!" said Riley, nodding his head. "I
thought so."

"What do you mean, Riley?" said Mrs.

Church, and Riley said: "I mean, I thought so because there isn't any such place."

"My goodness, how could you think she'd come from there, then?" Mrs. Church asked.

"Look," said Riley; "I'm Irish meself and I know Irish talk, and this person's imitation of Irish talk is the worst I ever heard, and I've heard some pretty poor ones and I know she ain't Irish. She ain't got the voice for it and she ain't got the face for it, for I've been watching her in the rear view mirror. And what's more, I think she's got an eye on your jewelry, and if I was you I'd tell me to stop the car and throw her out."

"My goodness!" said Mrs. Church, and she turned around and looked hard at Freddy. And then she began to laugh. "Drive right on, Riley," she said. "I know this old lady, and she's a friend of mine, and yours too." And she reached up and twitched the shawl back from Freddy's face. "I thought that cat looked familiar—how do you do, Jinx?—but I certainly didn't suspect who you were. What on earth are you doing out here?"

Freddy was disappointed. He had thought that his Irish dialect was pretty good. He had better not use it again. On the other hand, his disguise had worked all right with Mrs. Church, who knew him; it would certainly work with strangers. As they rode along he and Jinx told Mrs. Church where they were going and why. They told her the whole story.

"Well," she said, "I'll drop you in Tallmanville. I wish I could stay there with you and see what happens. But I'm going to a wedding in Washington and I have to be there tonight. I'm sure this would be lots more fun. But I'll be back in three days, and if your business is done by then I could drive you back home."

It was beginning to get dark when they reached Tallmanville.

"Where are you going to sleep tonight?" Mrs. Church asked.

Freddy said he hadn't thought about that. "But we'll find a barn door open somewhere," he said, "and curl up in the hay. We're used to roughing it."

But Mrs. Church said that wouldn't do, and she had Riley drive right up to the front door of the Tallman House, and she went in and engaged the best room for them. The hotel clerk was so pleased to have such wealthy guests that he didn't object when he saw that one of them was a cat, although there was a rule that no animals were allowed in the rooms. Mrs. Church went right up with them and punched the beds to see that they were soft, and looked out of the window to be sure that they had a nice view, and the clerk was so dazzled by her flashing jewelry that he blinked and bowed and rubbed his hands and promised that everything should be done to make them comfortable. Then Mrs. Church paid for their room and meals for three days, and said goodbye.

Chapter 5

As soon as the door closed upon Mrs. Church, Jinx jumped up on the bed and after trying both pillows with his paws, curled up on the softest one. "Boy, this is the life!" he said.

"You can sleep on that pillow later," said Freddy; "but right now we ought to go out and do a little scouting around."

"You go," said Jinx, and closed his eyes.

At that moment there came a tap on the door. Jinx, who knew that any cat, at any time, found in the middle of a bed was due for a licking, darted out of sight. Freddy pulled the shawl up higher over his ears and called: "Come in!" and the door opened and the clerk and the manager stood bowing and rubbing their hands on the threshold.

"Everything quite satisfactory, I hope ma'am?" said the manager.

"Thank you, my man," said Freddy haughtily. "It will do well enough, I fancy."

The manager bowed more humbly than ever. "I only wanted to suggest," he said, "that it might be wise if you kept your beautiful and no doubt very valuable cat in your room during your stay. You see, ma'am, there have been a lot of complaints in town lately about cats yowling and carrying on at night. There seem to be dozens of ownerless cats in town—I'm sure I don't know where they all come from, though when the mill closed a good many people left town, and I suppose they didn't take their cats along. Wicked, I call it, to abandon their pets that way. But that's how it is, and the town has had to appoint a cat-catcher to round up these animals and take them down to the pound. Of course I can see that your cat is a very highbred specimen, and not to be compared with these noisy alley cats—"

"I should think so indeed!" Freddy interrupted. "And I can assure you I have no intention of allowing my cat to associate with such riffraff. And now will you kindly leave us?"

When the door had closed again, Jinx said: "You'd better not be so uppity. That guy will throw us out on our ears if you talk to him that way."

"Don't you believe it," said Freddy. "He thinks we're important people."

"In that get up?" Jinx said. "Don't make me laugh. Take a look at yourself in the glass."

"Look," said Freddy. "We came in a big automobile with a chauffeur, and Mrs. Church came in with us all covered with jewelry. That's one reason why he thinks we're important. And another and better reason is because I'm wearing this torn dress and a threadbare old shawl. He thinks I must be even richer than Mrs. Church, because any friend of hers would have to be terrible rich to care so little what she looked like." Then he laughed. "Why he even thought you were a highbred cat!"

"That isn't very funny," said Jinx. "I'm just as well bred as you are, I guess. Huh! I guess—"

"Oh, shut up," said Freddy good-naturedly.

"We were both brought up by the Beans, and I guess nobody ever had any better bringing up than that. Look, Jinx, this business of all these stray cats gave me an idea. It's dark now, but it's only five o'clock. It's an hour or more before they'll bring our supper up to the room, the way Mrs. Church told them to. Do you suppose if you went out now you could get in touch with some of those cats? There's a porch under this window, and you could get out this way without going through the lobby."

Jinx said he could all right but he wasn't going to, and closed his eyes. Freddy knew there was no use trying to persuade a cat to do anything. He said: "All right, you stay here and I'll go. It'll be more fun than sitting around." And he put up the window.

"Oh, all right, all right; I'll go," said Jinx, jumping off the bed. "What do you want me to tell 'em?"

"Round up as many as you can," said Freddy, "and bring 'em back here. Don't tell them who I am—just say I'm an old lady who's fond of cats, and I want to invite them to supper. Don't let the clerk see you, and hurry up; you've only got an hour."

"You mean you're going to feed them our

good supper?" Jinx demanded. "Freddy, are you crazy?"

"Oh, don't argue!" said Freddy. "We've got to hurry. Get going, will you?" And he pushed the cat towards the window.

When Jinx had gone Freddy left the window up, although it made it pretty cold in the room, and then he arranged his shawl and went out. Mrs. Guffin's pet shop was on a side street, but he found it all right. Beside the front door was a big show window in which were five fox terrier puppies, and a lot of cages containing canaries. A sign said: Canaries. Your choice, 50¢. "That's pretty cheap for a canary," Freddy thought. He went up the steps and into the shop. A little bell on the door tinkled and after a moment a large unpleasant looking woman with a lot of bright yellow hair came out of a back room and said: "Good afternoon."

"Good afternoon," said Freddy. "What have you got new in animals?"

"New?" said the woman. "We haven't a very large stock at present. Are you looking for something for yourself? Something nice in fox terriers, now? I have a few left that I'm closing out at twenty dollars. Or if they are a little too expensive—"

"Expense is no object," said Freddy grandly. "I'm looking for a gift; something a little unusual."

"A canary makes a nice gift," said Mrs. Guffin. "Brightens up the home, I always think. I've priced these canaries at fifty cents for a quick turnover. Of course, at that price we don't guarantee them to be singers."

"That wasn't just what I had in mind," said Freddy. "This is a gift for a friend who runs a circus, and it ought to be something a little out of the ordinary. Say an anaconda. Or a leopard. You haven't a leopard, have you?"

Mrs. Guffin shook her head. "I haven't had a leopard in stock in I don't know when. And I never did handle snakes; there's not much call for them in Tallmanville." She hesitated, looking at Freddy sharply. "I might," she said slowly, "be able to get you something—something a little out of the ordinary run. It would be expensive—" Freddy waved aside the question of expense with one black-gloved trotter. "But if you are staying in town—"

"I shall be at the hotel for three days," he said. "Mrs. Vandertwiggen." That was the way Mrs. Church had signed for him in the hotel register—Mrs. J. Perkins Vandertwiggen and Cat.

"If you'll drop in tomorrow," said Mrs. Guffin, "I think I'll have something to show you. I'd rather not say anything more about it now— until I'm sure—"

"That's all right," said Freddy. He had been looking around, and his trained detective's eye had noticed several things that might have escaped an ordinary pig. He saw one thing in particular that told him just what he wanted to know. Mrs. Guffin wasn't a very good housekeeper and she hadn't swept the floor carefully. There were little heaps of fluff and dust in the corners of the room, and among them Freddy saw a number of long tawny hairs. They were too coarse to be human hair, and too curly to be horsehair. The only place Freddy had ever seen such hair was in Leo's mane, which was curlier than most lions' because Leo, every time the circus came to Centerboro, went into the beauty shop and got a permanent wave.

Another thing that Freddy had noticed was that one of the canaries in the big cage in the window kept winking at him. Every time he looked at the birds this one would squint up his

left eye in an evident effort to attract his attention. He went over to the cage and said: "I think
I'll take one of these canaries along."

"Pick out the one you want," said Mrs. Guffin. "Of course, you understand that at fifty
cents I can't guarantee that he'll sing."

"That doesn't matter," said Freddy. With the
black gloves which he wore to conceal the fact
that Mrs. Vandertwiggen had trotters instead
of hands, it was difficult to fish out a fifty cent
piece from the pocket of his skirt, but he managed it finally and laid the coin down on the
table. Mrs. Guffin was catching the bird he had
pointed out and didn't notice.

She said: "You'll want a cage for him. We
have a nice one at three dollars."

"I have a cage at home," Freddy said. "Just
slip him into my pocket."

Freddy didn't have a chance to talk to the
canary for some time. He couldn't talk to him
on the street, when the bird was in his skirt
pocket, and when he got back to his hotel there
wasn't much chance either, for his room was
full of cats. There were cats all over the bed, and
on the dresser, and in the chairs. There were
fourteen of them—big ones and little ones, black,
grey, tabby and tortoiseshell; and the only thing

they all had in common was thinness. They all looked half starved.

"My goodness!" said Freddy.

"Yeah," said Jinx disgustedly. "Well, here they are, and a pretty moth-eaten crew, if you ask me."

Several of the cats snarled angrily, and a big grey cat said: "Oh, is that so?" and crouched with his ears back as if about to spring at Jinx. But Jinx darted forward and gave him three swift cuffs—left, right, left—on the nose, and the grey cat backed off. Then Jinx walked around and distributed a few cuffs among the snarlers, who, as he knew perfectly well, were too weak to put up a fight. "You cats," he said, "will kindly remember that you are guests of Mrs. Vandertwiggen (smack) and we expect that you will behave (smack) like gentlemen. If you do (smack) we are delighted to have you with us, but if you don't (smack, smack) I personally will bat your ears down and heave you out the window."

The guests quieted down after this, and then Freddy addressed them. "My friends," he said, "I have asked you to dinner, and if you will be patient for a little longer the meal will be served. In the meantime I would like to say that I am in a position to provide those of you who are hungry and homeless with good places to live." And he explained about the mouse problem and the shortage of cats in Centerboro. "And now," he said, "will those of you who would like to go to Centerboro and be placed in good homes kindly raise the right paw?"

All the cats wanted to go, and Freddy was about to give them further instructions when there was a tap on the door. "Quick—under the bed, all of you!" he said. And when the door opened and a waiter appeared with a big tray of dishes, not a cat was in sight.

The tray had on it a large chicken dinner for Freddy and a big pitcher of milk and a bowl for Jinx. As soon as the waiter had set it on the table and gone, Freddy divided up the chicken and gave each cat a piece, and then Jinx let them take turns drinking out of the milk pitcher. While this was going on Freddy reached into his pocket and brought out the canary. The bird perched on the edge of the table and shook himself.

"About time you let me out of that place," he said crossly. Then he caught sight of all the cats. "Oh—oh!" he said. "This is no place for me." And he dove back into the pocket.

"We expect that you will behave (smack) like gentlemen."

But Freddy pulled him out again. "You'll be all right," he said. "Fly up there on the curtain rod over the window."

Twenty-eight cats' eyes followed the bird as he flew up and perched on the curtain rod. Thirty, if you count Jinx's. The grey cat said: "Aha! Dessert, hey? He'll top off the meal nicely." And he and two other cats started climbing right up the curtains.

But Jinx pulled them down. "I'm warning you guys," he said. "Any more rough stuff and you'll go out of here on your backs with your four feet in the air. You let that canary alone."

The bird leaned down and looked at Jinx out of his left eye. "Who's a canary?" he demanded. "I'm a chickadee; any fool can see that."

"Well, I guess I'm not a fool then," said Jinx with a grin, "because you look like a canary to me."

The bird fluffed up his feathers and hopped up and down angrily on the rod. "I'm *not* a canary!" he shouted—at least it would have been a shout if he had had a bigger voice; as it was, it was more a sort of buzz. He flew down to the top of the dresser. "I'm a chickadee," he repeated. "I'm dyed."

"You're what?"

"Say, are you dumb!" said the bird. "Mrs. Guffin has been dyeing us."

Jinx still didn't get it. He gave a loud laugh. "Dyeing you, hey? Well, you're killing *me*, so that's—" He stopped suddenly. "Dyeing you," he said thoughtfully. "Say, Freddy, do you hear that?"

"Yes. I thought it might be something like that," Freddy said. "That's why I bought him. You mean," he said to the bird, "that she's dipped you in dye?"

"Sure. She catches chickadees and tintexes 'em yellow and sells 'em as canaries at fifty cents apiece. That's why she won't guarantee that her canaries sing. We can't sing."

"How does she catch you?" Freddy asked.

"At her kitchen window. She keeps a chunk of suet on the sill, and when a few birds gather to eat it, she scoops 'em into the house."

The grey cat said: "She isn't the one that scoops 'em in. There's some kind of a big animal in there—"

"You're telling me!" the chickadee interrupted. "She's got a lion in there, chained up. He watches for the birds and grabs 'em. Fine business for a lion to be in, I must say! Picking on a lot of chickadees! Why don't he go out after ostriches? Why don't he tackle tigers and elephants? King of the beasts, he calls himself. Pretty cheap, if you ask me."

"H'm," said Freddy. "I don't get it. Any of you cats know anything about this lion?"

But none of them did. Most of them had caught glimpses at various times of some large person or animal with tawny yellow hair sitting in that window, but they hadn't cared to investigate.

"Well, we can't do anything about it tonight," Freddy said. "If this lion is who I think he is, I've got to get him out of there. Of course he may be some lion that really belongs to Mrs. Guffin. I'll have to figure some way to find out—"

"Well, what are you going to do about me?" the chickadee demanded. "Keep me here with all these cannibals? You think you've been so noble and rescued me—well, let me tell you I was safe in that cage, and I wish I was back there now."

"Oh, good gracious," said Freddy, "you're the most cantankerous bird, even for a chickadee, I ever saw. You can go home if you want to." He started to put up the window. "If you've got a home to go to."

"He watches for the birds and grabs 'em."

"Of course I've got a home," said the bird, "but how can I go back there like this? All yellow! Why, my folks won't even recognize me!" And he burst into tears.

"Oh, come on," said Freddy. "Come on into the bathroom, and I'll see if we can't scrub some of that dye off. Then you can sleep over the radiator tonight. I'll shut the door so the cats won't bother you. And in the morning when you're dry, you can go on home."

"And a good riddance," growled Jinx.

Chapter 6

The fourteen cats were pretty sleepy after the first good meal they had had in months, and they curled up in corners and on the dresser and in chairs and under the bed and slept peacefully all night. The chickadee, wet, but in his natural colors again, slept peacefully on the bathroom window sill over the radiator. And Freddy and Jinx slept peacefully in the big bed. It was the last bit of peacefulness any of them had for quite a while.

In the morning the waiter brought up a big breakfast. The cats hid under the bed again until he had left the room. After they had all eaten, and the chickadee had been sent off home, Freddy said: "Now you boys stay quietly here until Jinx and I get back. We're going over to have a look at that lion. I'm going to lock the door, but it's not to keep you in, it's to keep other people from coming in and finding you here."

There were quite a few people in the streets, but it was cold out, and nobody paid much attention to the little old woman and her black cat. They went around to Mrs. Guffin's, but when Freddy tried the shop door it was locked, and there was no answer to his knock. Then Jinx walked around to the side of the house and came back to report that there were fresh footprints leading from the back door out to the sidewalk. "She's probably gone downtown to do her shopping," he said. "I tried to get a peek in that window where she feeds the birds, but the shade is down. Look, Freddy, how do we know it's Leo she's got in there? We don't even know that it's a lion; it might be a lynx, or just a bobcat. My goodness, she tintexed the birds; she might have tintexed an old sheep and put him in the window. It doesn't seem to me that a big lion like Leo would be fooling around chasing a lot of chickadees."

"Well, there's one way to find out," Freddy said. "The way Richard Coeur de Lion's minstrel found out where Richard was imprisoned —remember?"

"How should I remember? I wasn't there."

"Well, you might have read about it."

"Pooh!" said Jinx scornfully. "I've got better things to do than read a lot of musty old books."

This was an old argument between them, but Freddy didn't want to start it up now. "All right," he said. "I'll just point out that here's one more example of something I read in a book that comes in handy. This minstrel didn't know where Richard was imprisoned, and he wanted to find out, so he visited castle after castle, and under the windows he'd sing a song that Richard would recognize. And at last one day Richard's voice answered him. He'd found him."

Jinx wasn't impressed. "I expect this minstrel had a good voice," he said. "But if you start singing, this lion or whatever he is will just think it's a fire engine siren, or maybe somebody having a fit, and he'll just put his fingers in his ears."

But Freddy went around and stood under the

window and sang the first few lines of a song
that he knew Leo would recognize. His voice
wasn't as bad as Jinx had pretended. It was a
light tenor which had a tendency to squeak on
the high notes, and he sang part of the Boomschmidt Marching Song which the circus animals used to sing when they were on the road.
He sang:

> "Red and gold wagons are coming down
>   the street,
> With a Boomschmidt, Boomschmidt,
>   boom, boom, boom!"

He stopped, and for a minute there wasn't
any sound. And then inside the house a husky
voice took up the song:

> "With shouting and music and tramp of
>   marching feet,
> And a Boomschmidt, Boomschmidt,
>   boom, boom, boom!"

The voice broke off, there was some thump-
ing, and then the window shade flew up, a large
tawny form was seen struggling with the window sash, and then it too flew up and the head
of a big lion came out.

"Leo!" Freddy exclaimed. "It *is* you then!"

"Why yes, ma'am," said Leo. "This is me. But—" He looked doubtfully at Freddy— "I don't think I've had the pleasure . . . Yet the voice is familiar . . ." And then as Freddy pulled the shawl away from his face, Leo let out a roar of delight. "Well, dye my hair if it isn't Freddy! And Jinx! Boy, am I glad to see you!" Then his voice dropped. "But you'd better get out of here. If that Guffin woman catches you—"

"Listen, Leo," Freddy interrupted. "You're the one that's got to get away from here. Can you climb out of the window?"

Leo shook his head. "I'm chained up. Big chain around my neck, and it goes down through the floor and around a big post in the cellar."

"Can't you pull it loose?"

"I might. But it would pull the insides right out of the house, and then how could I get away? Wherever I go I leave tracks in this snow, and the hunters would be after me again. I'm better off here, Freddy. And you're better off anywhere else. That Guffin woman—well, she isn't a nice person, Freddy."

"I talked to her yesterday," Freddy said. "She thinks I want to buy you."

Leo said: "Yeah. She's been dickering with a couple of zoos. She wants at least a hundred dollars for me."

"Oh, my land!" Freddy said. "I only brought a dollar and a quarter with me and I've spent fifty cents of that."

"There's nothing you can do," said Leo. "Thanks just the same. It was awful nice of you boys to come, and I appreciate—" He broke off. "Psst! Here she comes!" And he slammed down the window.

Freddy and Jinx got back to the sidewalk before Mrs. Guffin came along, but of course their tracks were visible under the side window, and when Freddy said good morning she looked at him suspiciously. "What were you doing out back?" she asked.

"W-well," Freddy said, "we—that is—I knocked, and then I thought you might be out in the garden so I went around back."

"Out in the garden in February?" she said. "What did you think I was doing—picking roses?"

Freddy pulled himself together and put on the haughty air that had gone over so well yesterday. "My good woman," he said, "I'm not in-

terested in your rose garden. I do not care for
roses, and I did not come here to purchase any.
I want—"

"I haven't *got* a rose garden!" shouted the
woman, and her big face got very red and angry.
"You said—"

"Please!" Freddy interrupted. "No need of
getting excited. I know what I said. I said I was
looking for you; it was you who began talking
about your roses. If you haven't any, so much
the better. I came to see if you were able to show
me the animal you spoke of yesterday."

The woman gulped and glared, but Freddy
had got her so mixed up about the roses that she
couldn't think of anything to say.

"I told you," Freddy reminded her, "that I
was looking for something unusual in the animal
line. Of course if you haven't anything, and are
just wasting my time—"

"I've got something all right," she said. "If
you've got the money to pay for it."

"I shouldn't worry about that if I were you,"
Freddy retorted loftily. "The name of Vandertwiggen is a sufficient guarantee of any amount
up to fifty million dollars."

Mrs. Guffin's features smoothed out. **The**

mere mention of any sum in the millions is often enough to smooth out even tougher features than hers.

But though he had advised her not to worry, Freddy was worrying some. He had started from home with just a dollar and a quarter in his pocket. He had spent fifty cents of it for the fake canary. He worked it out quickly in his head—he was rather slow at arithmetic, though —and as close as he could figure it he had somewhere around seventy cents left.

"What would you say," said Mrs. Guffin, dropping her voice, "if I told you I had a full-grown lion for sale? Ha, that's something unusual, I guess! That's something you don't just walk into a department store and pick up off the notion counter! That's—"

"Look," said Freddy, "suppose you show me your lion, and don't keep on telling me what he isn't."

"He'll cost you a hundred dollars," said Mrs. Guffin.

"All right, all right," Freddy said. "Show him to me."

So Mrs. Guffin took him into the shop. As he went in he bent down as if to pat Jinx, and whispered to him to stay outside to give warning if anybody came. "Now keep back," Mrs. Guffin said. "He's pretty fierce." And she opened the door into what seemed to be her diningroom. There was a big table, and a sideboard and chairs, and under the table on a blanket lay Leo. There was a brass collar around his neck, into which was padlocked a heavy chain.

Freddy sniffed. "Hmf! Pretty poor specimen. Where'd you get him?"

"Do you want him or don't you?" she said.

Freddy was thinking hard. If he had a hundred dollars . . . but he only had seventy-some cents. Yet if he said he didn't want to buy, he would have no excuse for coming back again. He hadn't planned his rescue very well.

He said: "I suppose you have a cage for him? I can't take him home like this."

"You'll have to provide your own cage," said Mrs. Guffin. "If you haven't got one, you can call up Johnson's hardware store. They may have a lion cage in stock; they have most everything." And she pointed to the telephone, which stood on a little table on the other side of the diningroom.

Freddy looked at Leo's chain. He saw that it was just about long enough to reach the little table. He wondered if Mrs. Guffin realized that.

"I never use the telephone," he said.

"You never *what*?" She stared at him. "You mean you—you don't know how? I never heard of such a thing!"

"I came here to buy a lion," said Freddy, "not to discuss my personal habits. If you'll kindly call the hardware store—"

Mrs. Guffin shrugged and went over to the phone. As soon as her back was turned Freddy winked at Leo, pointed at her, and made grabbing motions. Leo nodded, and when she had seated herself before the instrument he got up. He came out from under the table so quietly that not a link of the chain rattled. And then as Mrs. Guffin put the receiver to her ear, one huge paw came down on her right shoulder, and another huge paw came down on her left shoulder, and right at the back of her neck there was a deep rumbling growl.

Mrs. Guffin had nerve, all right. For a minute she didn't move, then she shuddered a little, and very slowly put the receiver back on the hook. She said quietly: "This won't get you any where."

Freddy said: "Where's the key to your pad lock, Leo?"

She said quietly, "This won't get you anywhere."

"In the pocket of her apron. But she's right, Freddy. There's no use my leaving here."

Freddy got the key and unfastened the collar. "Nonsense!" he said. "We'll lock her up and beat it. How can she stop us?"

"In an hour, half the population of Tallmanville will be out after us with guns," said Leo. "With this snow on the ground we can't hide our tracks. I could have got away any time in the last two months, but what was the use? I never should have tried to come north in the wintertime in the first place. As soon as I got into snow the hunters began to find my tracks, and they'd have caught me, too, if I hadn't happened to dodge in here just before Christmas."

Mrs. Guffin, with Leo's paws on her shoulders, had sat perfectly still—which seems like the sensible thing under the circumstances. But now she said: "If you really want this lion, Mrs. Vandertwiggen, you can have him for five dollars."

Freddy laughed. "He isn't yours to sell," he said. "He belongs to my friend, Mr. Boomschmidt."

"Never heard of him!" Mrs. Guffin snapped.

Freddy wasn't going to get into an argument. He walked around the room and tried several locked doors, but at last came to one which opened on a sort of pantry. There were shelves of dishes and supplies, and one small window, very high up. Freddy doubted if Mrs. Guffin could reach it; she certainly couldn't climb out of it. He took a chair in, and then told her to go in and sit on it.

She protested bitterly, but there wasn't much she could do. "You're just getting a dose of your own medicine," Freddy said. "How do you suppose those chickadees you trapped, like being shut up in cages?" They pushed her in and shut the door and locked it.

"Well," said Leo, "it's good of you, Freddy, to take all this trouble for me, but what good is it? I had a pretty tough time before I got here. After the snow began, and people began to notice my tracks, word got around that there was a lion roaming around the countryside, and I'll bet there were fifty hunters looking for me. I didn't leave tracks on the roads, but I couldn't travel on the roads because they could see me for miles against the snow. And at night the cars picked me up in their headlights. If I'd had any sense I'd have turned back south and waited for spring, but I don't know, I guess I'm sort of pig-headed . . . oh, gosh, excuse me, Freddy."

"Think nothing of it," said Freddy generously. "I don't know why it's so awful to call anybody pig-headed. Pigs—well, they're firm, they're determined, they don't just give up weakly when things go against them. If that's being pig-headed, then I'm glad I'm a pig."

Leo said: "Yeah. Well, you bear up under it well." He went on with his story. "I got up here to Tallmanville just before Christmas. The hunters were beginning to close in on me; they had me cornered in a little patch of woods just north of town. I knew I'd have to run for it, so I gave a couple of good loud roars up on the north edge of the woods, and then streaked it right down into the town. It was early morning; there wasn't anybody much around; and as I came down this street I saw this Mrs. Guffin shoveling a path around to her side door. She'd left her front door ajar and she had her back to me.

"Well, I didn't have any plan, but here was a place maybe I could hide. I was inside in two jumps, and I hadn't left any tracks on the clean sidewalk. I smelt food, and I came out here in the diningroom and ate up a loaf of bread and part of a pound of butter and some other things she had left over from breakfast. Then I heard her come in, and I got under the table. She came to the door and looked in, and then she gave a sort of grunt and said: 'Come out from under there.' So I came out.

"Well, she's got nerve all right. Most people, they come into the diningroom and find a lion there, and they give a yip and dive through the window. Sometimes they don't even bother about the yip. But she just said: 'H'm. I've heard about you. Hungry, I suppose.' And she went out in the kitchen and got me some more to eat. Then she said: 'You'd better take a nap while I think what's to be done with you.'

"I hadn't had much sleep for a week, and now with a good hot meal inside me I could hardly keep my eyes open. So I went back under the table. Next thing was, I woke up with this collar and chain on. I've been here ever since."

"Why did she keep you, I wonder?" Freddy said.

"She thought I'd escaped from a zoo, and maybe there'd be a reward. But she didn't have to chain me. I'd have had to stay—until spring anyway. This chain business made me mad."

"She was pretty good to you though, at that."

"Don't you kid yourself. Sure, she was good to me, if you mean she kept me alive. She had to keep me alive if she wanted to make any money out of me. But she fed me on stale bread from the bakery and bones from the butcher's. Bones are all right; I got nothing against bones. But she always boiled them first to make soup for herself, and a bone that has been made soup out of is about as pleasant to chew on as an old doorknob. Why, singe my whiskers, Freddy, I bet I've lost fifty pounds! I'm glad there isn't a mirror in this room; I shudder to think what I must look like."

"You look all right," said Freddy. "You're thin, and your mane is kind of faded out—probably from being indoors so much."

Leo said: " 'Twouldn't take long to get it in shape. A henna rinse would fix it up. And I ought to have another permanent; there isn't hardly a crinkle left in the darn thing, except at the ends." Then his head drooped. "But what's the use thinking about that? I can't get away from this place."

"Listen," Freddy said. "Mrs. Church brought Jinx and me down here in her car. She's picking us up again day after tomorrow and taking us home. Well, she picks you up too. You won't leave tracks riding in a car."

Leo cheered up a little at this news, but he

was still doubtful. What were they going to do until day after tomorrow? They couldn't keep Mrs. Guffin locked up; her friends and neighbors would begin to wonder . . .

"You leave it to me," said Freddy. "We'll work it somehow. Right now I have to go back to the hotel. I'll leave Jinx with you." And he went to the door and called the cat.

"Hi, lion," said Jinx. He looked at Leo critically. "Boy, you certainly look like a candidate for the Old Lions' Home. You look like you've been entertaining a couple of moths. What's the matter—didn't a diet of chickadees agree with you?"

"You've heard about that, eh?" said Leo. "I didn't eat the chickadees. But I had to catch 'em for her. She dyed them and sold them for canaries. Nights I hadn't caught any I didn't get any supper. But eat 'em!" He made a face. "Oh, I was hungry enough to, but they don't pay for the trouble. You're picking feathers out of your teeth for the next hour."

Jinx said: "Yeah. I gave up birds years ago. Feathers tickle your nose and make you sneeze so you can't tell what you're eating. Mice now— they're real tasty. But I gave them up too. I like 'em personally, you understand, and it don't seem right to eat 'em. Kind of abusing their friendship, isn't it?"

Freddy had adjusted his shawl and was moving towards the door. "You two stand guard over Mrs. G. while I'm gone," he said. "I'll hurry back. And better lock the front door after me, so if anybody comes they'll think Mrs. G. is out shopping."

Chapter 7

Back at the hotel Freddy went up the stairs and down the corridor towards his room. He was just fumbling in his pocket for his key when he heard a terrified scream, the door of his room was flung open, and a chambermaid came tearing out, her eyes wild, her skirts flying. She galloped past Freddy without even seeing him and made for the stairs, screaming all the while.

Freddy thought: "Oh, gosh, I forgot that the chambermaid would have a key. She's gone in to make the bed, and seen the cats." And that, as he found later, was what had happened. If you go into a room and see one cat there you don't think anything about it. But if you go in and fourteen cats all turn around and look at you, you can be excused for screaming a little.

But Freddy realized that something had to be done, quick. Fortunately nobody looked out of any of the other doors on that corridor; the guests were evidently all out. But downstairs he could hear shouts and commotion and the chambermaid's excited voice explaining to somebody. "Send for the cat catcher," somebody called. And another voice said: "Better take a club, Joe."

There was an empty laundry hamper at the far end of the corridor. "Hey, you cats; come out here quick!" Freddy called through the doorway; and as they trooped out he raised the lid of the hamper. "Jump in—all of you!" And as they hesitated: "The cat catcher is coming!" That and the footsteps pounding up the stairs decided them. Freddy tucked in a couple of tails, slammed down the lid of the hamper, and leaned nonchalantly against it.

Practically everybody in the hotel—clerk, manager, cook, waitresses, chambermaids, guests—came piling up the stairs, and, all talking at once, crowded into Freddy's room. Nobody noticed the little old woman down at the end of the corridor—which was lucky, for there was a good deal of snarling going on inside the hamper, which hopped and jumped around and generally behaved as if someone was setting off fireworks inside it. And then when everybody had got into the room, Freddy quietly ran up the hall and quietly closed the door and locked them in.

Then he threw up the hamper lid. "Quietly, now—quietly!" he said. "Be quick and follow me closely, and I'll get you out of this."

The cats were scared, and they followed without making any fuss. He led them down through the lobby and out a side door into an alley behind the hotel. They followed this down until they were opposite the street where Mrs. Guffin lived without seeing anybody. Then, when nobody was in sight, they made a dash for the pet shop.

There was some delay when Freddy knocked, for Leo was upstairs washing his mane. He came down with his head a white froth of soapsuds and unlocked the door. The cats were nervous when they saw him, but they all came in, with the exception of a scrawny brindled cat named Louis, who ran off and never came back.

Freddy was a little cross with Leo. "You ought to be keeping an eye on Mrs. Guffin," he said, "instead of beautifying yourself. She could break down that door."

"Oh, I suppose you're right, Freddy," said the lion. "But my mane was in terrible shape."

"Well, you finish washing it in the kitchen," Freddy said. "There's a spray on the faucet there, and I'll help you. We have to hold a council of war." He started to tell them what had happened, but Leo said: "Help me first, Freddy. I'll catch cold standing around with this soap on."

So they went out in the kitchen. Leo held his head over the sink, and Freddy put the spray on and began rinsing out the soap. And of course got soapsuds in Leo's eye. Leo let out a roar that could have been heard half a mile. He roared and shouted and shook his head, and the soapsuds flew all over the kitchen, and the spray was knocked out of Freddy's grasp and soaked Jinx, who had been looking on with a superior grin. Jinx gave an angry screech, and the thirteen cats, who were sitting around in the shop, yowled in sympathy, the way cats do, and the puppies

And, of course, got soapsuds in Leo's eye.

barked, and even the birds set up an excited twittering. Altogether there was enough noise to bring every neighbor in the block to the front door.

It took some time to get everything quieted down. The soap had made the kitchen linoleum so slippery that nobody could stand up on it, and after Leo had tried to rinse his own head and had slipped and fallen down and cracked his chin on the edge of the sink, he went back upstairs to finish. Freddy rubbed Jinx down with a dish towel, and then he wiped the suds off his shawl and hung it up to dry.

It was while he was doing this that there was a loud knock at the front door.

"Darn that Leo!" said Jinx. "He's stirred up the whole neighborhood." He went into the shop and came back to report that there were two women on the porch, and a third was trying to peer into the shop window.

Freddy went to the pantry door and spoke through the keyhole to Mrs. Guffin.

"You'd better keep pretty quiet, ma'am," he said. "If you make any noise I'll unlock the door and sick this lion on you. And you know—well, he hasn't had much to eat lately."

He turned back to see Leo, with a bath towel

tied round his head, standing behind him. The lion said reproachfully: "That isn't a very nice thing to suggest, Freddy. You know I'm not that kind of a lion. Besides," he added, "even an alligator would have to be pretty hungry before he'd tackle her."

A voice outside called: "Yoo-hoo, Mrs. Guffin! Are you all right?"

Freddy had an idea. There was a blue bathrobe of Mrs. Guffin's lying across a chair, and he grabbed it up. "Quick, Leo! Up on your hind legs and get into this. Now if we had a handkerchief . . . a dishtowel will do; get one, Jinx."

A minute later, Leo, wrapped in the bathrobe, with the dishtowel draped over one paw, which he held across the lower part of his face, opened the door a crack and peered out at his neighbors. "What's all the excitement?" he said in a hoarse whisper.

One of the women said: "Are you all right? We heard all that racket, and thought—"

"What racket?" Leo demanded.

"We thought it came from over here. Yells and shouts. Are you sure you're all right? You look queer."

"Got a bad cold," said Leo. "Mustn't stand here in the draught."

"What's the matter with your voice?" asked another woman. And the third one said: "Have you sent for the doctor?" "You were all right this morning when you were sweeping the porch," said the first.

"These things strike sudden," whispered Leo. "One minute you're up—next minute you're down. Hurts me to talk; go away and leave me alone, will you?"

"Well, if that's the way you feel!" said the first woman indignantly, and the second one said: "We only wanted to help you." "That's gratitude for you!" said the third. And they turned away.

"You were pretty rude to them, Leo," Freddy said.

"They'd have been suspicious if I'd been polite," said the lion. "She hasn't got any more manners than a—" He stopped abruptly.

"Oh, go on, say it," said Freddy. "Than a pig —wasn't that what you started to say? I don't know why people always have to bring pigs into it when they want to say something mean about somebody. If somebody's stupid and obstinate, why don't they call him lion-headed? If somebody's rude, why don't they say he has no more manners than a cat? Why—"

"Look, Freddy," Leo interrupted. "It's just one of those sayings; it doesn't mean anything. Like 'fierce as a lion,' 'bold as a lion.' I'm not any fiercer and bolder than you and Jinx. And 'curious as a cat.' Jinx isn't any more—"

"Yes, I am too, more curious than you are," Jinx said. "That's why I know more: I'm more curious, and so I find out more things. Those old sayings are all right. 'Clever as a cat,' 'cute as a cat,' 'courageous as a—'"

"Conceited as a cat—that's a better one," said Freddy. "Listen, we've got to decide what to do. Mrs. Church won't be back for us until day after tomorrow. We'll have to keep Mrs. Guffin locked up, but we can't make her sit on that chair in the pantry for two days. That's cruelty to humans. But if we let her stay in her bedroom, she'll go to the window and yell for help."

They talked it over. They didn't want to be any meaner to her than they had to, and they at last decided that she would be locked in the pantry during the day. At night she could sleep in her own bed, but Leo would be locked in with her. Then if she tried to call the neighbors, the lion could stop her. "And don't you worry," he said. "I'll sleep right under the window, and if she tries any funny business—" He crouched and lashed his tail, and began to creep towards Freddy with a ferocious grin.

Freddy backed away. "Hey, quit that!" he said. "I—I don't like it!"

The lion didn't move a muscle. He stared at Freddy with his fierce yellow eyes, and then suddenly he twitched his whiskers, and Freddy jumped convulsively backward and fell over a chair.

When he scrambled to his feet, Leo was sitting up and looking at him with a pleased smile. "My goodness," Freddy said, "you looked awful, Leo! I've known you so long, I've sort of forgot you really are a lion."

"That's all right," said Leo. "I just wanted to show you that I'm not going to let Mrs. Guffin forget it. We won't have any trouble with her."

"I guess she won't sleep much," said Jinx.

"Oh, I won't bother her if she behaves herself. Just give a little growl now and then to remind her I'm there." He stopped suddenly and they all raised their heads to listen. Somebody had knocked at the front door.

"You'll have to go, Leo," Freddy said. "Here, get into your bathrobe again."

Freddy and Jinx stayed in the diningroom. They heard the bell tinkle as Leo opened the door, and they listened. But Mrs. Guffin had heard the bell too, and suddenly she began to yell at the top of her lungs: "Help! Help! Police! I've been kidnaped!"

"We've got to put a stop to that!" Jinx said. He rushed at the door between the diningroom and the shop and slammed it, and Freddy put his mouth close to the keyhole of the pantry door. And when Mrs. Guffin stopped for breath, he called to her. "One more yell and I'll let this lion in at you."

But she didn't mean to be silenced so easily. Freddy heard her draw in a deep breath for another yell. "Here, Leo!" he said. "Go in and get her! Chew her up!" He rattled the doorknob, then dropped down and put his nose to the crack under the door and made the sort of snorting, snuffling sounds that he supposed a lion might make if he was trying to get at somebody.

Mrs. Guffin didn't use her breath for another yell. Freddy heard her let it out in a sort of sigh. "All right, Leo," he said quickly. "I guess she doesn't want to be eaten up after all." Then he answered for Leo with a deep growl. There was a good deal more pig than lion in it, but I guess it fooled Mrs. Guffin for she didn't yell any more.

In a few minutes Leo came back. "Some man

wanted to buy a canary," he said. "I told him to stop by next week. I said I was too sick to keep the shop open today."

"Well, but didn't he hear Mrs. Guffin?" Jinx asked.

"Sure. I told him it was a parrot." Leo laughed. "He said he'd like to buy the parrot; he'd never heard one with such a deep voice. Maybe we could sell Mrs. Guffin to him."

"I wish we could," Freddy said. "She can do a lot of hollering in the next two days. I wonder . . ." He thought a minute, then he went and rummaged in Mrs. Guffin's desk and found pen and ink and a piece of cardboard and lettered a big sign: MEASLES, which he hung in the shop window. "That ought to keep people away," he said.

It did keep them away too. During the rest of that day several people came up on the porch, but when they saw the sign they went away again without knocking. Fortunately there was plenty of food in the house, and at noon they let Mrs. Guffin out of the pantry long enough to get something to eat for herself. Leo sat close beside her while she ate. He didn't growl any, but now and then he would draw his lips back from his long sharp teeth in a sort of silent snarl as he watched her. She didn't seem to have much appetite.

When they had locked her up again they had their own lunch, and they fed the thirteen cats and the puppies and birds in the shop, and then Freddy walked back to the hotel. When he went in, the manager was talking to the clerk. He glanced up and frowned. "Ah, Mrs. Vandertwiggen, we've been looking for you."

Freddy said, very haughty: "Well, my good man, here I am. State your business."

The manager rubbed his hands together but he didn't bow. "Well, ma'am," he said firmly, "it's about the cats. I'm afraid I shall have to ask you to leave. We can't allow you to fill your room with cats."

"I don't know what you are talking about," said Freddy. "I understood you had no objection to my having my cat with me. He should be in the room now, but he can hardly be said to fill it."

"I am not referring to your cat," said the manager, and he told Freddy what had happened. "It caused a great deal of disturbance, and a great deal of running around and yelling, and we don't like that here. This is a respectable hotel."

Freddy said: "Nonsense! Did you see these cats?"

"No, ma'am. But—"

"Be quiet!" said Freddy sharply. "You didn't see them. Nobody saw them, except the chambermaid. Yet you came right upstairs when she screamed. Where did they go to then? Do you mean to tell me that they vanished into thin air?"

"They must have gone somewhere," said the manager.

"If they ever existed," said Freddy. "And you say when you went up there there were *no* cats in the room? Where is my cat, then? He is an extremely valuable animal, and if you have let him get out—if he's lost . . . Kindly come up to my room with me at once."

So the manager went up, and of course Jinx wasn't there. "Well," said Freddy, "this is serious for you—very serious indeed. I think I see what happened. You allowed my cat to get away, and to cover up your carelessness you invent this story of a roomful of cats. I shall call my lawyer at once."

The manager began to look worried. "Well, ma'am," he said, "perhaps I was a little hasty. I shall question the chambermaid again. I hadn't thought of it like that, but it seems possible that she may have done as you say. If so, she shall be discharged at once."

But this wasn't what Freddy wanted at all. He became even more haughty than before. "I'm afraid," he said, "that you can't pass off your own stupidity and carelessness on to an innocent person. However, I do not wish to be too hard on you. I will overlook the whole thing, provided you agree to say nothing to the chambermaid. My cat is not stupid, and he'll come back when he gets ready."

So the manager agreed. When he was gone Freddy locked the door and dropped down into a chair and wiped his forehead on the corner of his shawl and said: "Whew!" And by and by when he felt calmer, he got pencil and paper out of his pocket. And he wrote a poem. This is it:

Men call the dog the friend of man
  And praise him for his deep devotion,
And yet the pig is capable
  Of love as deep as any ocean.

"Bold as a lion," people say,
  "Strong as a horse"—pigs too have strength
And in defense of justice, they
  Will go to almost any length.

Yet who has ever heard it said
　　That pigs are brave, that pigs are bold,
That pigs are handsome quadrupeds
　　With wills of iron and hearts of gold?

"Fat as a pig" the saying goes;
　　"Pig-headed," "dirty as a pig";
Each reference, in verse or prose,
　　To pigs contains a dirty dig.

I demand justice for the pig!
　　No more shall he be stigmatized
By adjectives, both small and big,
　　So vulgar and unauthorized.

O pigs, arise and prove your worth,
　　Assert your honesty and charm;
Let kindly, clean and polished pigs
　　Abound on every ranch and farm.

Let "pig" no longer be a word
　　Applied with snorts and sniffs and jeers;
Let pigs be proud of being pigs
　　As peers are proud of being peers.

Justice! Justice for the pig!
　　Let every pig in every pen
Lift up his voice, assert his rights
　　As one of nature's noblemen.

Chapter 8

Freddy stayed at the hotel that night and went back in the morning to the pet shop and spent the day there. Mrs. Guffin didn't cause them any trouble. She looked tired and sort of depressed, which I guess was only natural for anyone who had spent the night in a room with a lion; and she said frankly that Freddy could have Leo for nothing if he'd only take him away; all she wanted was to be rid of them. But they kept her locked in the pantry just the same. The "Measles" sign kept any customers away from

the shop, but Freddy thought it was queer that
none of her friends called, if they knew she was
sick.

Leo said: "She hasn't got any friends."

"Not any at all?"

"Well, none that ever come to see her."

"I thought everybody had *some* friends,"
Freddy said.

"Not her. Listen, Freddy; one day there was
a woman came, and when she saw Mrs. Guffin
she held out her arms and said: 'Why, Gwetho-
linda Guffin! Well, well, you look just the same
after all these years!' But Mrs. Guffin just folded
her arms and said: 'Who are you?' 'Why, don't
you remember your old schoolmate, Mary
What'sis?' says the woman. 'Well,' says Mrs.
Guffin, 'what of it?' 'Well, dear me,' says the
woman, 'I thought you'd be glad to see me, because I just got back to Tallmanville after being
in Chicago so long, and we were such good
friends.' 'Well, you could have stayed in Chicago
for all of me,' says Mrs. Guffin, and the woman
just stared at her a minute, and Mrs. Guffin says:
'Well, what do you want? I've got to get back to
my housework.' So the woman just turned
around and went."

Freddy said: "Tut, tut!" At least he made the

clicking sound with his tongue that is always written "Tut, tut," in books because you can't really spell it. If he had said: "Dear me, how dreadful!" it would have meant the same thing, and I wouldn't have had to explain so much. Anyway, that's what he did, and he said: "That's certainly no way to keep friends."

"Maybe Mrs. G. was mad because her friend told her she looked the same after all these years," said Jinx. "Golly, don't you suppose she's changed at all? She must have been a pretty tough looking little girl."

But later in the day they came across a photograph album, and in it Jinx found a picture of Mrs. Guffin, aged nine. She looked just the same, only smaller. They all looked at it and said, "Tut, tut, tut!" And then they shut the album and put it away. It wasn't anything you could really figure out.

Freddy spent that night in his hotel room again, but didn't go back to the pet shop in the morning. He didn't think Mrs. Church would get there before afternoon, but he didn't dare take the chance of missing her, so he sat in the window and watched the street. And about two o'clock Mrs. Church's big car drew up before the door. Freddy ran down, and when he had explained all that had happened, they drove around to the pet shop.

On the way home, Leo sat in the back seat between Mrs. Church and Jinx, and Freddy sat in front beside Riley. The thirteen stray cats were tucked in wherever there was room. Some of the dyed chickadees, whom Freddy had released from their cages before leaving the shop, flew along beside them for a mile or two, diving and turning somersaults in the air, and putting on an acrobatic show for them. In the back seat, as the car whirred along up the snowy road, Mrs. Church listened with interest to the story of Leo's adventures. Freddy tried to talk to Riley, but the chauffeur was unaccountably grumpy; he answered with nods and grunts, and refused to be drawn into conversation until Freddy asked him right out what was the matter.

Riley screwed his face up into an expression of deep gloom. "Look," he said; "I'm hired to do what Mrs. Church wants me to do. I ain't kicking; we get along fine. If she says: 'Drive to the moon'—O K, we drive to the moon. But there's some things she hadn't ought to ask."

"You mean like driving Leo and Jinx and me?" Freddy asked. "You mean you don't like having animals in the car?"

Some of the chickadees flew along putting on an acrobatic show for them.

"No, no; you know I don't mean that," Riley said. "It's these cats."

"You mean there are too many of them in the car?"

"There's either too many or too few, according to how you look at it. There's thirteen, ain't there? Well, that's bad luck."

"Oh," said Freddy, "I see. You mean you're superstitious about it. Well, but look here; there's fourteen, if you count Jinx."

"Yeah. Just the same there's thirteen, if you don't count Jinx."

"That doesn't—excuse me, Riley, but that doesn't make sense to me. My goodness, you can't help being superstitious about the number thirteen, but you don't have to count everything in thirteens, do you? I mean, if you go buy a dozen cookies, and carry them home in a paper bag, do you figure that's thirteen things you're carrying—twelve cookies and one bag?"

"Gosh, I never thought of that," said Riley. "Well, I suppose I could eat one of the cookies."

"You'd be carrying it just the same—inside you," said Freddy. "You can't beat it that way."

Freddy knew that you can't stop people being

superstitious by telling them how foolish they are. They know they're foolish all right. They say so themselves. "I know it's foolish," they say, "but I think it's bad luck to spill the salt." Freddy knew this because he was superstitious about some things himself—only not about the number thirteen. But he tried to argue with Riley.

Everybody in the car got into the argument finally, and it went on a long time. Each one apparently had a pet superstition which he took seriously, while making fun of everybody else's. One of the cats told about a man he used to live with who thought it was such bad luck if he got his shirt, or even one of his socks on wrong side out when he was dressing, that he would put his pajamas on and go back to bed again in order to get up again and start the day right.

"The trouble with believing that certain things bring bad luck," Mrs. Church said, "is, not that they really do bring it, but that you believe they do. In believing it, you sort of prepare the way for bad luck. It's like riding a bicycle— if you expect to fall off, pretty soon you do. But if you just go ahead and ride, without thinking much about it, you don't have any trouble."

"Yeah?" said Riley. "How about the other

day when you made me park in front of the Methodist Church?"

"That proves what I just said," Mrs. Church replied. "Riley's superstitious about parking in front of a church," she said, "and in town the other day the only empty space was in front of the church. He wanted to go on and come back later, but I said no, he'd have to park there. Well, he got so nervous worrying about bad luck while he was trying to get the car in close to the curb, that he stepped on the accelerator instead of the brake and ran into the car in front, and smashed a fender and it cost me thirty dollars."

"What I don't understand," Freddy said, "is why we're always superstitious about things that bring *bad* luck. Why can't we be superstitious about *good* luck? I mean, instead of thinking it's bad luck when you spill the salt, why not think it's good luck when you spill the pepper?"

"Because it wouldn't be," said Riley. "People would go around knocking over the pepper as often as they could, and everybody'd sneeze all the time. That ain't good luck."

"I see what you mean, Freddy," said Mrs. Church. "We ought to look for good signs instead of bad ones. You ought not to go around being scared all the time; you ought to be hopeful. But I can't think of a single thing that's supposed to be good luck.—Oh yes, I remember one: if you drop a fork, it means company is coming."

"That ain't necessarily good luck," said Riley. "It depends on the company."

They all tried to think of things that were signs of good luck coming, but none of them could. "Just the same, there must be some," said Mrs. Church. "If, as they say, coming events cast their shadows before them, good things ought to cast just as long shadows as bad things."

I don't know why none of them thought of four-leaved clovers.

It was after dark when they reached the Bean farm, and Mrs. Church only stopped a few minutes to say hello to Mrs. Bean, and to Mrs. Wiggins, who was a great friend of hers. Then Freddy and Jinx thanked her and she shook hands all around with everybody including the thirteen cats, and drove off.

The next morning Freddy got Mr. Bean's permission and he hitched up Hank to the cutter and he and Leo drove into town. He dropped Leo at the beauty parlor and went on to the newspaper office, where he wrote out the following advertisement.

HAVE YOU GOT MOUSE TROUBLE?

Are mice disturbing your sleep, destroying
your property, and scaring your
wife and children into fits?

CALL FREDDY, THE POPULAR DE-MOUSER

Let our staff of trained operatives mouse-
proof your home. Charges reasonable.

All work guaranteed.

FREDDY; *at the Sign of the Fleeing Grey Mouse,
Bean Farm, R.F.D. #2, Centerboro.*

He had this put in the paper and then he drove over to the bank, where he found Mr. Weezer not too pleased with the results of the suggestions he and Jinx had made. The trouble was that news of the free cheese offer had got around town, and on Thursday—which was the day the cheese was given out—the bank mice had had so many guests from outside that Mr. Barclay had had to go out three times for more cheese, and even then it wasn't enough. "This bank is the strongest bank in the county," Mr. Weezer said; "it has enormous resources, it has weathered eight depressions. But it cannot afford to buy cheese for all the mice in town. And even if it could, it causes too much disturbance. You could hear them scampering around and squeaking even up here—you wouldn't believe that mice could put on such a noisy party. And once a lot of them came right upstairs from the vaults and played tag all over the place. They chased Miss Gillespie right up on top of her desk, and of course she screamed. I don't suppose you can blame her, but it doesn't look well to have an assistant lady cashier hopping around on the desks and squealing during banking hours. The people outside the cage couldn't see the mice, of course. They just thought—well, goodness knows what they thought. Several of them closed out their accounts at once."

Freddy said he was very sorry. "But I have a better scheme now," he said. And he told Mr. Weezer about it. "I'll bring the cats in and chase every mouse out of the bank."

"Chasing them out is one thing, but keeping them from coming back is another," Mr. Weezer said.

"I'll leave one cat on guard to see that they don't come back," said Freddy.

Mr. Weezer thought that might work. "But what are you going to charge me?"

"Nothing," said Freddy. "We've caused you a lot of trouble, and the least we can do is straighten it out. But what do you think we ought to charge other people? Do you think a dollar a house would be too much?"

"Not nearly enough," said Mr. Weezer. "Five dollars a house, Freddy. For one thing, it's worth it; and for another, you'll get more people at five dollars than you would at one. I don't know why that is, but it's so. The less you charge for your services, the less people seem to want them. And there's another thing: half of the houses in this town are overrun with mice. If you go about it right, you can make enough to get that circus you were talking about back on the road again."

From the bank Freddy went over to the beauty parlor, but Leo wasn't ready to go home. He was still sitting under the dryer with his eyes shut, and one of the young ladies was putting red nail polish on his claws. She looked up when Freddy came in. "I don't like this job much," she said. "If this lion wasn't a friend of yours—"

"Why there's nothing to worry about," said Freddy. "Leo wouldn't hurt anybody."

"Maybe not," said the girl. "But why does he growl all the time then?"

Freddy listened. Above the hum of the dryer

he could hear a regular harsh snarling noise. It sounded like a heavy truck trying to get out of a snowbank. He laughed. "He's purring," he said.

Leo opened one eye. The dryer made so much noise that he couldn't hear what they were saying, but he smiled at Freddy. "Hi, pig!" he said. "Wait till you see how I'm having my mane done. Miss, will you show him the picture? Like to see what you think of it."

The girl brought a book containing pictures of various kinds of hair-dos, and turned to one which showed the hair pulled up tight from the back into a sort of plume on top. Of course it was not a picture of a lion but of a pretty girl, and it was hard for Freddy to imagine what it would look like on Leo.

"It's that fashionable up-sweep," said Leo. "The latest thing. I think it will be becoming, don't you?"

The girl said to Freddy: "I wanted him to have something more conservative. This would look all right on a movie star, but—"

"He thinks he looks like a movie star," Freddy said.

"They all do," said the girl.

"What's that?" Leo asked, trying to hear.

"We think it's very smart," Freddy shouted. "Very becoming."

Leo gave a satisfied nod and closed his eyes again. And Freddy went over and sat in a chair and composed a poem.

"Some people think pigs should feel pain
Because they're so awfully plain,
But they don't, and the reason
Is easy to seize on:
Being handsome's a terrible strain.

If you're handsome, you're always ob-
sessed
With a doubt you're not looking your
best,
And then you get worried
And hurried and flurried
And spill things all over your vest.

Whereas, if you're homely as sin,
You just have to bear it and grin,
For no perseverance
Will improve your appearance;
You're beaten before you begin.

It is no use to sit down and squall
If you can't be the belle of the ball;

If you're cross-eyed and fat
You just say: 'That's that!'
And you don't have to worry at all.

Now the pig, as I previously said,
About looks never worries his head.
The pig has no passion
For being in fashion
And painting his fingernails red.

And that is why pigs are so gay,
Always laughing and shouting Hooray!
Their looks they ignore;
They don't care any more;
And they sing and rejoice all the day."

When he had finished writing this, Freddy got up and looked at himself in one of the big mirrors. He frowned, he turned his head from side to side, and then he smiled and examined his teeth. And then he opened his eyes wide and looked interested.

"H'm," he said. "Ha! Not bad!

"Lions!" he said. "Pooh!"

And then he went back and tore the poem he had just written into little pieces and dropped them in the wastebasket. That is why you will look in vain for this poem in The Complete Poetical Works of F. Bean.

Chapter 9

Freddy's anti-mouse advertisement in the paper had immediate results. The first day after the paper came out he had twenty-eight requests for his services in the mail. He borrowed Hank and the cutter again and drove the thirteen cats into town. Jinx refused to go with him.

"I don't approve of this business, Freddy," he said. "If it was rats we were going after it would be different. I wouldn't mind taking a hand and knocking over a rat or two myself. But I've got too many mouse friends to feel right about chasing these mice out into the snow."

"They're just a lot of gangsters," said Freddy. "Destroying property and chewing holes in people's Sunday suits."

"That may be so," said Jinx, "but there ought to be some way of getting rid of them without declaring war on them."

"All right, you think of a way," said Freddy. "In the meantime, I'm going ahead. We've got to raise that money for Mr. Boomschmidt, Jinx."

Freddy knew that if you've got something to sell, you've got to be as conspicuous as possible. He had printed a sign on cardboard and fastened it to a stick. It read:

'Twas the night before Christmas, and all
    through the house
Not a creature was stirring, not even a mouse.

DO YOU KNOW WHY?

Because FREDDY, the POPULAR DE-MOUSER had been called in the day before.

He left Hank and the cutter at the edge of town, and then he and the cats marched up Main Street to the bank. Freddy came first, carrying the sign. Behind him was the big grey cat, whom he had appointed foreman, carrying a smaller sign, which read:

LET US TAKE THE SQUEAKS
OUT OF YOUR PANTRY

Then, in single file, followed the twelve other cats. There had been no time to provide uniforms for them, as Freddy would have liked to do, but each one had a blue ribbon around his neck, and from the ribbon hung a pasteboard key tag on which Freddy had drawn the trademark he had thought up: a mouse, running away. And the last cat carried another sign:

You Can Have a Mouseless House, Too
Only $5

The people lined up on the sidewalks and laughed and cheered as the little parade went by, and several people rushed out with five dollar bills in their hands and Freddy put their names down in a little book. Then he marched the cats into the bank, and down into the vault.

There was a few minutes of squeaking and scampering downstairs, then the cats marched up and the foreman saluted and reported the bank clear of mice. Freddy left one cat on guard, and led his crew up Main Street. Nearly every house on upper Main had requested the de-mousing service, and he divided his crew into squads of three and sent them into the different houses. By noon he had de-moused twenty-two homes, two groceries, and a barber shop, and had earned, as closely as he could figure it, some-where around a hundred and twenty dollars.

When the noon whistles blew, he and the cats went into Dixon's Diner and had a good nourish-ing lunch of hamburgers and milk, and then they went to work again. At five they knocked off for the day and Freddy counted up his money. He had earned $291. Where that extra dollar came from neither he nor anyone else ever fig-ured out.

Of course with only thirteen cats it was im-possible to leave one on guard in each house to prevent the mice from coming back. But Freddy had thought of that. He had given three of the cats armbands, on which were inked the letters: M.P. (for Mouse Police) , and these M.P.'s were to patrol the neighborhood during the night. When he had given them their orders, he met Hank, who had been waiting for him at the livery stable, and drove back home.

Freddy was pretty pleased. At this rate, he'd soon have as much money as he needed. The cats were staying in Jinx's studio, and when he had left them he went over to the cow barn. He could hear several animals talking as he came up to the door, but the talk stopped as soon as he went in. The three cows were there, and Robert, the collie, and the four mice—Eek and Quik and Eeeny and Cousin Augustus. The cows and the dog nodded to him, but the four mice turned their backs.

Freddy frowned and looked from one to the other of his friends, and then he looked at the four small grey backs. He thought they looked very stiff and indifferent. Then he said: "Am I intruding? If I've interrupted a private conversation—"

"You're very kind and polite, aren't you?" said Eek sarcastically, without turning round. "We're not speaking to you!" Eeny snapped.

Freddy tried to pass it off as a joke. "You're not?" he said. "But you just did."

"Don't say anything more to him, Eeny," said Quik.

"But if you won't say anything to me," said Freddy, "how can I find out what is the matter?"

"Will you kindly tell your friend," said Eeny,

He and the cats went into Dixon's Diner and had a good nourishing lunch.

addressing Mrs. Wiggins, "that he knows perfectly well what is the matter."

"Certainly," said Mrs. Wiggins, and turning to Freddy: "The mice feel that you know perfectly well what is the matter."

"Oh well, yes," said Freddy; "I do, I suppose. I mean, it's because I've gone into the anti-mouse business, isn't it? But my goodness, these mice in Centerboro aren't like you boys. They used to be pretty well behaved. They stuck to crumbs and no squeaking after ten P.M. and no chewing the furniture and so on. But this last year they've just sort of gone wild. There's always room for a few well-behaved mice in a house. But now there's hardly room in the houses for the people that own them."

"Aw, Mrs. Wiggins," said Eeny, "tell your friend that that's all a lot of baloney. Those poor Centerboro people," he said sarcastically; "my heart bleeds for them! Being pushed around and crowded out of their homes by a lot of ferocious mice! But of course we know why he's doing it. It's the money. Anything for a few dollars. Friendship, honesty, decency—nothing means anything except piling up some more dirty money!"

"Oh, baloney yourself!" said Freddy crossly.

"Sure I want the money. And you know why. You know the trouble Mr. Boomschmidt is in."

"And how about the trouble our Aunt Sophie is in?" demanded Quik. "Ask him about that, Mrs. Wiggins. She's lived in Centerboro all her life, at Miss Halsey's. Always been a quiet, unassuming little body and never did any harm to anybody. Sends us cards every Christmas and on our birthdays, as regular as clockwork. And now in her old age I suppose she's to be driven out into the snow to starve."

"It's a conspiracy, that's what it is!" Cousin Augustus shouted. "Why doesn't this big bully pick on dogs? Or cows? Why persecute the mice? I'll tell you why: because mice are small and weak and can't fight back. Sure, never mind the rights and wrongs of the case; bring in a gang of roughneck cats and we'll have a lot of fun pushing the mice around!" Cousin Augustus made quite a speech. He waved his paws around and shouted like a senator, and once he forgot that he wasn't speaking to Freddy and turned right around and faced the pig, until Eeny put a paw on his shoulder and swung him back towards Mrs. Wiggins. Freddy couldn't get a word in edgeways. But at last Cousin Augustus ran down, and Freddy said:

"There's something in what you mice say, no doubt. As for your Aunt Sophie, she is all right, because Miss Halsey hasn't hired us to de-mouse her house yet. But let me point out a few facts to you. Those mice in Centerboro are really driving people right out of their houses. And something had to be done. If I could have thought of any other way, without bringing in the cats—"

The mice all began talking at once, but Freddy shouted at them. "Shut up! What's the use of sitting around calling names? Let's get an independent viewpoint; let's hear what Robert and the cows think."

The four animals appealed to looked at one another. Then they went over to the other side of the barn and held a conference. They muttered together for a while, and then came back and Robert said: "Offhand, we can't think of any solution that will satisfy both parties. We don't think the mice ought to be allowed to run wild in Centerboro. On the other hand, we don't think they ought to be driven out into the cold and the snow. We have only one suggestion: that a fact-finding committee be appointed, one member to be selected by Freddy, one by the mice, and a third impartial member to be agreed on by both sides."

"A good idea," said Freddy. "I'll select myself for my representative."

"And I'll select *my*self," said Cousin Augustus.

"Then I'd suggest," said Mrs. Wogus, "that for your third member someone like Old Whibley be named. He's honest, and wise, and he won't take six months to come to a decision."

After some arguing, this was agreed to, and as it was important that some decision be reached before the cats raided any more houses, Freddy, instead of going into Centerboro the next morning, set out on his skis for the woods where Old Whibley lived. To keep himself warm during the conference he wore an old tweed suit of Mr. Bean's, and Cousin Augustus rode in the pocket.

Chapter 10

It was pretty hard going up across the pasture towards the woods, for although the slope wasn't steep, there was an icy crust on the snow, and Freddy was not really an expert on skis. He dug in his ski poles and puffed and panted like a steam engine, and indeed he looked a good deal like a steam engine, for with every puff a little plume of white steam blew out of his nose into the frosty air. Cousin Augustus, who was riding in Freddy's pocket, stuck his nose out from time to time to see what progress was being made, but he didn't say anything because he still wasn't speaking to Freddy.

When he got up to the duck pond Freddy stopped to rest. The pond was frozen solid under its thick snow blanket, and the little house where the ducks lived was just a bump on the edge of the pond. But a little path went into a tunnel at one side of the bump which Freddy knew went to the front door, and a faint haze of smoke above the bump showed that Uncle Wesley was keeping a good fire up in the stove which Mr. Bean had put in the duck house two years ago. Alice and Emma came down to the barnyard nearly every day, but Uncle Wesley felt the cold, and so he stayed home and stoked the fire.

"I suppose we ought to stop in and call," Freddy said. "But maybe we'd better not. You know how Uncle Wesley is: once he gets talking it's a day's work to get away from him."

Cousin Augustus didn't say anything, just gave a couple of mouse snorts and ducked back into the pocket.

"Ho, hum!" said Freddy. "You're not very good company, Gus." He picked up his ski poles and went on.

He had got up to the edge of the woods when a faint sound made him stop and listen. At the same moment Cousin Augustus poked his head out of the pocket and listened too.

"Did you hear something?" Freddy asked.

Cousin Augustus just gave him a dirty look and went on listening.

"Oh, all right," said Freddy disgustedly. "Be stubborn then. I just asked a civil question."

Just then the sound came again. It was a faint flat little voice, and it said: "Help! Help!"

"Where'd it come from?" Freddy asked. "You've got better ears than I have, Gus." And then as the mouse didn't answer, he shrugged his shoulders and started down along the fence.

Cousin Augustus was determined not to speak to Freddy, but he didn't see why he shouldn't talk to himself. So he said to himself in a loud voice: "If this fool pig had any sense he'd climb the fence and look behind that big elm." And then he answered himself and said: "Quite right, Augustus; that's where the call came from. But of course it's too much to expect of a great hulking stupid lummox like this Freddy that he'd ever get anything right."

So Freddy climbed the fence, and sure enough, behind the elm he found a small brown duck, apparently entangled in a lot of snow-covered brushwood.

"Hey!" he said. "What's the matter—what are you doing up here? Why, I know you; you belong to Zenas Witherspoon, over the hill."

"Yes," said the duck weakly. "I was just—er, taking a walk, and I got my foot caught, and before I could get free—well, I got so cold I couldn't feel my feet, and then I didn't know how to get loose."

"I see," said Freddy. "Taking a walk. Two miles from home. Admiring the view, no doubt. Of course, all you can see is our duck pond, but . . . H'm, aren't you the fellow that sent that clever valentine to Alice and Emma?"

"If you want to get out of here, duck," said Cousin Augustus, "you'd better make this pig a cash offer to help you. He isn't as stupid as he sounds. He's crazy about money, and he's just working around to finding how much you've got. If you can't pay, he'll leave you here to freeze to death. Though probably he'll make a real sad poem about you afterwards, if that's any consolation."

"Oh, shut up!" said Freddy. "For two cents I'd dump you right out here, Gus, and let you do the freezing."

This was an unwise remark, and Cousin Augustus took immediate advantage of it. "There, you see?" he said. "Two cents—that's his price. For as little as two cents he'd throw an old friend out in the snow and let him freeze."

Freddy didn't say any more, but he leaned down and worked the duck's feet loose from the entangling branches. But the duck's toes were evidently frozen, for when he tried to walk he just fell over.

"Can't take you over to Witherspoons'—it's too far," Freddy said. "I guess I'll put you inside my coat and carry you down to the duck house."

"Oh, dear!" said the duck. "Oh I *don't* want to go down there! Couldn't you—couldn't you just leave me here?"

"Don't be silly," said the pig. "What's your name?"

"Edward."

"Well, Edward, cruel and vindictive as I am, I am not going to leave you up here to freeze, just to save you from the embarrassment of being brought face to face with the two good ladies who are the objects of your divided affection—"

"Making fun of a poor frozen duck!" put in Cousin Augustus, twitching his whiskers commiseratingly. "That's what you can expect from

"There, you see?" he said. "Two cents—that's his price."

this brute, Edward. Well, you have my sympathy."

"Oh, dear; oh, dear!" Edward moaned, as Freddy tucked him inside his coat. "I shall die of shame; I shall simply die of shame!"

"Nonsense," said Freddy. "What is there to be ashamed of? You sent Alice and Emma a very clever valentine. You stated—I presume sincerely—that you found them both very attractive, so attractive that you couldn't decide which one you would like to marry."

"Oh, I never said a word about marriage!" Edward protested. "Not a word! I wouldn't presume—"

"Suit yourself," said Freddy. "Probably neither one of them would have you, anyway. But at least you ought to make up your mind which one you prefer, and if you stay there for a few days, until you're well enough to go home—"

"Stay there!" Edward interrupted. "You mean, trespass on their hospitality, push myself in—"

"I'm the one that's pushing you in," Freddy observed.

Edward was appalled at the idea. He was sure that Alice and Emma would think that getting his toes frozen was all a fake, just a pretext to get him inside their house as a guest. He moaned and lamented all the way down to the pond, begging Freddy to abandon him, to let him just quietly die without any fuss. Even Cousin Augustus got pretty fed up with him before Freddy poked his ski pole down the little tunnel and knocked with it at the ducks' door.

There was an excited quacking under the snow, and pretty soon Uncle Wesley came bustling out. He was a fat, pompous little duck, greatly admired by his nieces, who thought he knew all the answers. Of course they didn't put it just that way. They said he was a very profound thinker. Nobody else on the farm thought he knew much of anything.

"Well, my young friend, good morning," he said. "Good gracious, what have you there?"

Freddy explained, and produced Edward, who was so embarrassed that he kept his eyes tight shut. "His toes are frozen," Freddy said. "He's in no condition to go home, and I thought—"

"Quite right, quite right," said Uncle Wesley "Job for the girls. They're fine nurses, you know. Alice! Emma!" he called. "Come out here." Then he shivered. "Brrrrr! You'll excuse me,

Freddy; this air is a little sharp for my neuritis. The girls will see to this fellow." And he hurried back into the house, as Alice and Emma came out.

They looked at Edward, who, with his eyes still closed, was being held upright by Freddy. Then they looked at each other.

"Why, Alice; I do believe it's—"

"Ssssh! But it certainly is, sister! Dear me!" Alice giggled faintly.

"Are—are his eyes—" Emma began.

"Just bashful," said Freddy. "He was hanging around—that is, he says he was taking a walk up above here and stayed out too long. Froze his toes."

"Oh dear, the poor boy!" Emma quacked. "Can he—no, I see he's too weak to walk. We'll help him into the house. Alice, put his wing over your shoulder."

Supported by his wings over the others' shoulders, Edward was squeezed into the tunnel. Before they disappeared, Alice said: "We'll take care of him. And thank you, Freddy."

"Yes, Freddy," said Emma. "Thank you very much."

Freddy went on up into the woods. He knew the big tree, high up in which Old Whibley, the owl, had his nest; and when he came to it he rapped on the trunk with a ski pole. Almost at once a harsh voice called: "Stop that racket!" and looking up, Freddy saw the owl's big square head at the door of the nest.

"Excuse me," said the pig. "We've come up to see if you would be willing to act as chairman of a fact-finding committee on the mouse situation."

"Certainly not," said Old Whibley. "Fact-finding indeed! Have more facts now than I know what to do with. Why find more? If you want 'em, go find 'em yourself. I've no use for 'em."

"Well, that's just a name for the committee, really," said Freddy. "Actually, we have all the facts. What we'd like to do is present them to you and have you act as judge."

"I don't want to find 'em and I don't want 'em presented to me. I tell you I don't care a hoot for all the facts there are. Not one hoot." And he gave a hoot to show Freddy how little he cared.

"All right," said the pig. "I suppose we'll have to get Uncle Solomon, then; though we'd much rather have you."

Uncle Solomon was a screech owl, and he was probably about the last person any of the ani-

mals would want to have as judge, because while
he was very learned, he never cared much about
the rights or wrongs of an argument. All he
cared about was the argument itself. He loved
arguing. He loved it so much that often if he
found he was winning, he would change sides
quickly and start agreeing with the people he
had been talking against a minute before. It was
bad having him against you, but it was almost
worse having him on your side.

"Tcha!" said Old Whibley disgustedly. "You
might as well ask the weathercock on the church
steeple to be your judge. Get four different answers in ten minues."

Freddy had only mentioned Uncle Solomon's
name in order to keep Whibley talking. If he
could get the owl interested, he was sure he
would take the case.

"Uncle Solomon is very wise," he said.

"He knows a lot. 'Tain't the same thing."

"He's an awful smart arguer."

"Tcha! Argument ain't wisdom. Take your
Mr. Bean—he don't ever argue. Doesn't say
hardly anything. Just decides what he wants
done without any talk—snip, snap!—all decided.
And he's a wise man."

"Oh, yes; he certainly is," said Freddy.

"I guess so!" said the owl. "I guess so! And that's what I say—arguing isn't any good. Never convince anybody by argument. Just make 'em more set than ever." He fluffed out his feathers and stared with his enormous yellow eyes at the pig. "Why don't you get Mr. Bean to judge?"

"Well," said Freddy, "we—we wanted you."

"Tcha! Nonsense!" snapped Old Whibley. But he was pleased all the same. And in a minute he said: "Well, state your case. Haven't got all day."

So Freddy told him quickly about his anti-mouse campaign, and then Cousin Augustus came out and sat on Freddy's shoulder and stated the case for the mice. When he had finished, Old Whibley asked some questions. Was there a head mouse in Centerboro—anybody in authority. Freddy said he didn't think they were organized.

"Always easier to deal with an organization," said the owl. "However . . . What do you figure would be the cost of food per day per mouse?"

"The what per what?" said Cousin Augustus, looking puzzled.

"I thought you had your facts!" Whibley snapped.

"He means, how many mice could you feed

for a week on, say, a ten cent loaf of bread," said Freddy.

"What's that got to do with it?" Cousin Augustus said irritably. "My goodness, we come here for your help and you ask us riddles!"

"All right, all right," said Old Whibley huffily. "If that's the way you feel. I wash my claws of the whole affair." And his head disappeared from the doorway.

"Now you've done it," said Freddy. "Why couldn't you answer him?"

"I didn't come here to do arithmetic," said the mouse.

"You came here to answer any questions Whibley asks you," said Freddy. "That is, if you want his help in this business."

"Well," said Cousin Augustus slowly. "Only I didn't see . . . Well, I suppose about twenty mice." And then he called out the answer to the owl. And he said: "I'm sorry I was rude. I just couldn't think—"

"Don't try," said Old Whibley, appearing again at his doorway. "You're not used to it, and you'll get us all mixed up. Got a pencil?"

Neither of them, of course, had one.

"Just have to do it in our heads then," said the owl. "Won't be easy. But first, how many mice do you figure there are in Centerboro, Freddy?"

Freddy said it was hard to tell. But he'd guess at least four thousand.

And how many people did he figure there were who would pay him five dollars to have their houses de-moused?

That was hard to tell, too, but Freddy would guess that there were five hundred.

"Say four hundred," said the owl. "Makes our problem easier. Now you can expect to take in four hundred times five; that's—h'm, ha! He scratched his ear. "How do you figure it, pig?"

Freddy took his ski pole and scratched the figures on the snow:

$$\begin{array}{r} 400 \\ 5 \\ \hline \$2000 \end{array}$$

"Good," said Whibley. "Tidy sum, two thousand dollars. But now, suppose you take that money, but instead of driving the mice outdoors, you rent a hall somewhere for 'em to live in, and feed 'em until spring. Say two months more. What would that cost you?"

"My goodness, I don't know," said Freddy.

"I didn't suppose you did. But we can figure it. Now first you've got to rent a hall. I suppose a good tight barn would do. For two months. What would that cost?"

"Twenty dollars," said Cousin Augustus.

"Sure of that figure?"

"Yes, sir. At least, that's what Mr. Bean paid one year for one of the Macy barns, when he wanted to store some extra hay."

"Ten dollars a month? I think your Mr. Bean got stung, but that's his affair. Say twenty dollars then. Good. Now you've rented your hall. And that leaves you—"

Freddy marked on the snow:

$$\begin{array}{r} \$2000 \\ -20 \\ \hline 1800 \end{array}$$

"Sure that's right?" said Old Whibley. "Well now, if it costs ten cents to feed twenty mice for a week, how much will it cost to feed four thousand mice for two months?"

Freddy saw what the owl was getting at, and he went to work with his ski pole. He was not a really good mathematician, and he covered all the snow within twenty yards of the tree, but he finally worked it out that if it cost ten cents to feed twenty mice for a week, it would cost twenty dollars to feed four thousand mice for the same time, and a hundred and sixty dollars to feed them for eight weeks. It took him some time, and once he got into fractions by mistake and had to stop and smooth the snow out and start over again. Then he put down:

$$\begin{array}{r} \$1800 \\ -160 \\ \hline 1540 \end{array}$$

which of course was wrong, but it was near enough, and Old Whibley didn't notice it either.

"My, that's fine!" Freddy said. "I'll have over $1500 for Mr. Boomschmidt, and the mice will be taken care of. If that's agreeable to you, Gus."

Cousin Augustus said grumpily that it was better than nothing. At least the mice wouldn't starve or freeze. "But at the best," he said, "it's nothing but a concentration camp. And you're making a lot of money out of it. How about cheese twice a week?"

"That's all right," said Freddy. "No reason why we couldn't give them cheese, and an occasional cake, maybe, and even put on a little entertainment for them now and then. Only they'll have to agree to stay in the barn—not go sneaking back into the houses."

"You get your barn," said Cousin Augustus.

"And then you call off your cats and take me and my brothers into Centerboro and let us arrange it."

Freddy said: "OK. I'll turn my de-mousing orders over to you. You can go in instead of the cats, and move the mice out. But I'm going to keep my M.P.'s on for a while just the same, to patrol the town."

They argued about this for a while, but Freddy was determined, and at last the mouse agreed. They looked up to thank Old Whibley, but the owl had gone back inside and closed his door.

Chapter 11

The scheme Old Whibley had suggested worked out to the satisfaction of everyone concerned. Freddy found a barn he could rent on the edge of town and then he took Eek and Quik and Eeny and Cousin Augustus down, and sent them into the houses to sell their plan to the mice. With few exceptions, the town mice agreed to move into the barn and stay there till spring, for no sensible mouse is going to turn down three square meals a day, with cheese twice a week and no cats.

Freddy could have moved the mice over into

the barn quietly without any fuss, but that was
not his way of doing things. So one day when he
was all ready he ran big advertisements in the
Bean Home News and the Centerboro paper.
They read:

THE PIED PIPER OF CENTERBORO
Will free your town of mice
Monday, at 2 P. M.

Watch for Him! Wait for Him!

Corner of Main and Elm
2 P. M., Monday

Don't miss the big parade!

By half past one that Monday, Main Street
was jammed with spectators. Everybody in town
was there, and the sheriff had even brought all
the prisoners down from the jail to see the show.
At five minutes of two Freddy appeared. His
friend, Miss Peebles, who had a millinery store
on Main Street (maybe you've seen the sign
yourself: *Harriet—Hats. Latest Paris Cre-
ations*) , had helped him with his costume. He
had on a peaked hat with a peacock feather in it,
and a long coat, sewn all over with tags of vari-
colored ribbon that fluttered as he moved. At
two o'clock sharp he pulled out a tin fife that he

had bought at the Busy Bee store and started up Main Street, tootling the first seven notes of Yankee Doodle—which was all of it he could play—and as he passed each house the mice came tumbling out and followed along behind him, dancing and squeaking. They were pretty excited, for few of them had ever been in a parade before. Some of them formed a conga line which wound up on to the sidewalk, and even went right up one side of the square bank building, and across the roof, and down on the other side. Eeny always said afterwards that the leader was his Aunt Sophie, but when they asked her she just said: "Certainly not!" and tossed her head. And I hardly think it was so, for Aunt Sophie was a quiet, retiring person, even for a mouse, and anyway she was much too old for that sort of thing.

Of course some people who were afraid of mice were frightened. Old Mrs. Peppercorn was so scared that she swarmed right up the trellis on to Judge Willey's porch, and they had to get the fire company to get her down. But she wasn't hurt, and she said afterwards that she wouldn't have missed the sight for anything. "And I wager I saw it better than anybody else in town," she said.

Freddy's M.P.'s patrolled for a week, but as none of the mice seemed to want to get back into the houses, he withdrew them. He had no further use for the cats now, and as they were a noisy and quarrelsome crew he advertised that anyone that didn't live in Centerboro could have one by calling for him, and he got rid of all of them in two days.

Of course Freddy now had a lot of money. He had $1726. If it had been summertime, he would of course have kept it in his own bank, of which he was president. But the First Animal Bank was closed for the winter under a snow-drift seven feet deep, so he deposited it in the Centerboro bank.

He hadn't written to Mr. Boomschmidt be-fore, because he didn't want to say anything about getting the circus on the road until he was sure he could help. But now he wrote. He told about Leo and Jerry, and about the money he had earned, and he said that if Mr. Boomschmidt could get his animals together and wanted to take up the circus business again he would lend him the money. He would have sent a check for the whole amount right then, but he was afraid that Mr. Boomschmidt would not take it as a gift. That was why he spoke of lending it.

In about ten days he got an answer:

Dear friend Freddy:

I take my pen in hand to reply to yours of the 26th inst. I am very glad you are well and all the other good friends at the Bean farm. I am happy that Leo and Jerry are with you and not in any trouble. We are all in good health here. As to what you propose, it would be quite a job to round up all our old performers. Hannibal and Louise are in the zoo in Washington, and Rajah is in Louisville, but most of the others are I don't know where, though now and then I get a picture postcard from one or another from some distant point. Still, I suppose we could find some of them. The wagons and tents and everything are stored here and are all in good shape. Your old friend Bill Wonks is with me still, and Madame Delphine who told your fortune once, she says, and her daughter, Mlle. Rose, and of course my dear mother, who is still knitting me those fancy waistcoats—ha, ha, Freddy, you remember those waistcoats, I guess. Well, I tell you Freddy that is a pretty fine generous offer of yours to lend me that money, but good gracious Freddy suppose the circus did not do well and I could not pay you back? I know you would not care if I lost your money, but I would care, and so I am going to say no. But I tell you what I will do. I will go into partnership with you. You putting up the money, and I putting up the know-how and the equipment. How would you like to be a circus man? I think you would make a good one. You think it over Freddy and write me. If you say yes I can start getting things ready.

Give my love to Leo and Jerry. I miss Leo a good deal, and I suppose I must miss Jerry too, now I come to think of it. Hoping this finds you and all the good friends at the farm in good health as it leaves me,

Sincerely your friend,

Orestes Boomschmidt.

Freddy took the letter into the stable to show to Leo. The lion was in the box stall next to Hank. He had borrowed Jinx's mirror, and he spent most of his time in front of it, turning his head this way and that and admiring his new hair-do. He turned towards the pig with a slightly discontented expression on his face.

"Give me your frank opinion, Freddy," he said. "What do you think of the way I had my mane fixed?"

Freddy thought it was pretty ridiculous, pulled up tight from the back and piled in a sort of heap on top. But of course he didn't say so right out. He stepped back and frowned and

put his head on one side and one fore trotter up
to his chin to show that he was thinking deeply.
Then he walked slowly around his friend. Once
or twice he nodded as if agreeing with himself,
and once or twice he shook his head in disagree-
ment. And at last he said:

"Well, it's very smart, Leo. Very fashionable.
But I think just a *leetle* extreme. I think dignity
would be the keynote for lions, and this is just a
trifle, just a *mite*, undignified."

Leo nodded. "Afraid you're right. There was
two juncos flew in here this morning; asked me
if I'd rent 'em a nest in it. Smart alecks! If I could
have got a paw on 'em—"

"That's the trouble with style," said Freddy.
"Everybody naturally wants to wear the latest
thing, but the latest thing isn't always becoming
to everybody. Personally, I just let fashion go.
Because I'd look funny in any of the new styles.
If I wash behind my ears, and don't slouch, that's
about as far as I care to go."

Leo nodded. "You always look nice," he said.
He looked at himself again in the mirror and
then began combing his mane with his claws.
"I'll get these hairpins out and comb it down
over my shoulders again. That's really the most

effective arrangement. Ripples nicely, don't you think?" Then he looked at Freddy. "What have you got there?"

So Freddy showed him the letter. "That's a nice offer of Mr. Boomschmidt's," he said, "and it would be a lot of fun running a circus, being on the road. But I'd have to be away from the farm all summer. I don't want to do that."

"He won't use your money unless you go into partnership with him," Leo said.

"Suppose I give you the money and you go into partnership with him," said Freddy.

"Uh-uh," said Leo. "Oh no, thank you most to pieces. My Uncle Ajax always used to tell me: never have money dealings with your friends. There's nothing that breaks up friendship as quick as money. Why I could tell you cases—"

"Sure, sure," Freddy interrupted. "But that doesn't help me any. I've got to find some way to get him to take that money. I wish he wasn't so proud."

"All the Boomschmidts were proud," said Leo. "I remember my Uncle Ajax telling me about our Mr. Boomschmidt's father, Ulysses X. Boomschmidt, when he had the circus. He was so proud that when the show was over and people were coming out, if he heard anybody

"But I think just a leetle extreme."

say they hadn't enjoyed it, he'd rush right up and give them their money back. Sometimes he'd even give 'em a dollar extra—'to pay you for the time you've wasted,' he'd say with a low bow. Sometimes, when the applause hadn't been very loud during the show, he'd get thinking that maybe nobody had enjoyed it, and he'd give everybody their money back. Finally it got so he paid out lots of times more than he'd taken in, because some people would come out of the big tent two or three times. If the old man hadn't retired, the show would have gone bust."

"That's very interesting," said Freddy, "but it still doesn't help. I guess I'd better go down and talk to Mr. Weezer."

It wasn't a very good day to go to Centerboro. Although it was well along in March, the long awaited thaw had only just begun. But it had begun in earnest. A warm rain was melting the snow and turning the fields to ponds and the road to a river. Freddy hadn't been able to persuade Hank to take him down in the old phaeton. " 'Twon't do my rheumatism any good to get my feet wet," the horse said. So Freddy borrowed Mrs. Bean's second best umbrella and splashed off down the road.

It wasn't a very good day to get advice, either.

Mr. Weezer gave one of his rare dry laughs when he heard Freddy's problem. "It's a very unusual case," he said. "Mostly people come to consult me about how to get money *out* of other folks' pockets without their noticing it—not how to put it in. I don't see what I can do, Freddy; it's completely out of my line." He shook his head thoughtfully. "If you want to start up the circus, I guess you'll have to accept the partnership."

"I can't let Mr. Boomschmidt down," said Freddy. "I'd better draw my money out and start for Virginia right away, then."

"If you get into any difficulties, remember the Centerboro bank is behind you," said Mr. Weezer. "We're all pretty grateful to you for the mouse job." He got the money in crackly new twenty dollar bills, and Freddy tucked it into the inside pocket of the old coat.

"Won't it be pretty dangerous, traveling with all that money?" the banker asked.

"Nobody'd rob a pig," Freddy said. "Besides Jerry and Leo are going along; nobody would tackle them."

He thanked Mr. Weezer and went over to the jail. The prisoners felt pretty bad when they heard that Jerry was going to leave them. They had made a saddle for him, and on good days

they took turns riding him around the jail yard.
The sheriff didn't want them to take him out on
the road until they had found some way of steering him, for his mouth was so tough that an ordinary horse bit was no good—a strong man, pulling on the rein, couldn't pull his head around;
and his eyesight was so poor that he was always
running into things. One of the prisoners had
got badly bruised when Jerry had run full tilt
into a large elm tree.

Jerry was glad to be going back to Virginia,
and so was Leo. " 'Tisn't that I don't like it here,
Freddy," the lion said. "You've treated me fine
—taken me right in like one of the family. But
Mr. Boomschmidt is going to need me. And then
. . . well, I've been here six weeks, and you
know, my Uncle Ajax used to say that a week
was long enough to visit anybody. In a week you
can say all you've got to say; after that you begin
repeating yourself and telling your stories over
again. Uncle Ajax said that if you didn't get
thrown out, you at least wore out your welcome."

"Nonsense," said Freddy; "you could stay
here all your life and not wear out your welcome.
But we've got a lot of work waiting for us in
Virginia. I'd like to wait till the roads dry out,

but I guess we ought to start tomorrow morning."

That afternoon Freddy walked up to the duck pond. It had stopped raining, and the snow was nearly all gone from the pasture, and all around him as he went squelching up the slope, the whole hillside chuckled and chirped with running water. Uncle Wesley was sitting by his front door, shivering a little and looking very glum, and when he saw Freddy he got up and came to meet him.

"I know you're going to say it," he said gloomily. "But I wish you wouldn't."

"Say what?"

" 'Fine weather for ducks.' So many people feel they must say that when it's wet, and I can't tell you how tired I am of it."

"I wasn't going to say anything of the kind," said Freddy. "I just dropped in to see how your patient was getting on."

"Hoo! That Edward!" said Uncle Wesley disgustedly. "Will you believe me, my friend, when I tell you that that wretch has so insinuated himself into the good graces of my dear nieces that their old uncle is no longer of any account in his own home? Sits there like a—like a king, in *my* house, and allows them to lavish on him all the little attentions that should be the due of their devoted uncle, who has repeatedly sacrificed himself for their welfare. All my little comforts —the down cushion in front of the fire—'Edward must sit there, dear uncle; he doesn't feel well.' 'Edward must sleep now, uncle; we must be quiet.' Even the guest room has been given to him. I sleep in the kitchen! The kitchen! Me!

"Ah, ingratitude, ingratitude!" Uncle Wesley declaimed. "It has made me a stranger in my own home!"

"Why don't you throw him out?" Freddy asked. "You're bigger than he is."

Uncle Wesley nodded his head slowly. "I have thought of that," he said. "Yes, even I, who have always preached that violence in any form is vulgar and inexcusable, have been tempted to use force. But I cannot but feel that a dignified forbearance is the only course open to a gentleman. The example I have given my nieces, the standard I have set for them, has been a high one. I cannot bring myself to be guilty of conduct which I have taught them to condemn. Even at the cost of my comfort—yes, of my self-respect, I must not lower myself in their eyes."

"You seem to have got yourself pretty well lowered anyway," Freddy said. "Personally, if

things are as you say, I'd have a lot more respect
for you if you pulled some of this fellow's tail-
feathers out."

Uncle Wesley smiled condescendingly. "Yes,
you would think of that. But I have never yet
cared to win a cheap notoriety by acts of vulgar
violence."

Freddy said: "Yeah?" and grinned. And just
then Edward, followed by Alice and Emma,
came out. And certainly, Freddy thought, the
roles had changed. For now it was Alice and
Emma who simpered bashfully, while Edward
acted almost as self-important as Uncle Wesley.

"Good morning, Freddy; good morning,"
said Edward. "I was just going to escort Cousins
Alice and Emma down to the barnyard. First
day we've been able to get out. Shall we go down
with you?"

" 'Cousin,' eh?" Freddy thought. "Well,
well!" He said: "Sure, we'll go on down."

Uncle Wesley moved away and stood on the
bank, looking down at the water with dignity
and an occasional shiver, while Edward, with
Alice on one side and Emma on the other, pre-
ceded him down the hill.

"I suppose you've quite recovered from your
frostbite, Edward?" Freddy said.

Edward stopped. "You girls go along," he said. "We'll follow you." He fell in beside Freddy. "Sure," he said. "I'm all right now."

"Got your eyes open, anyhow," said Freddy with a grin.

The duck said: "Nice little house the girls have here, isn't it? Lots nicer than the coop I have at Witherspoons'."

"Very nice," said Freddy drily. "Made up your mind which one you want to marry yet?"

"Oh, that!" Edward said. He looked doubtfully at the pig, then gave a chuckle. "Frankly, old chap, I've rather given up the idea of marriage. You see, if I do say it that shouldn't, they've got very fond of me. And if I chose one, d'ye see, the other would be pretty disappointed. I hate to give pain. So-o-o,—well, I thought I'd just stay on for a while as a guest. They've given me a very nice guest room and bring me my breakfast every morning. We're all cousins together—a happy family, you might say."

"So I might," said Freddy. "But you're **Mr.** Witherspoon's duck. Won't he want you back?"

"You know old Witherspoon—how tight he is," said Edward. "If I'm getting three meals a day that he doesn't have to pay for, he'll be satisfied. No, Freddy," he said seriously, "they've really adopted me as a cousin, and it's pretty nice having a family. I was brought up by a hen, you know—always had to play with chickens—had no brothers or sisters, no family life at all."

"I suppose that was what made you so bashful," said Freddy. "You seem to have got over it pretty well."

"That's a funny thing, Freddy. I don't say I've got over it entirely. But when folks are as nice and considerate as Alice and Emma are,—well, your bashfulness kind of goes away."

Freddy wondered if Edward had really been as bashful as he made out, but he didn't say so. When they got down to the barnyard, Alice and Emma took charge of their new cousin, and took him to call on all their friends. They would introduce him, and then they would stand back and admire him, nodding proudly at each other every time he opened his bill to say "Pleased to meet you," as if he had uttered words of the most profound wisdom. They treated him, indeed, very much as they had used to treat Uncle Wesley, in the old days before they had found out what a pompous old fraud he really was. But what really bothered the animals was the way they fluttered and tittered. They acted downright silly.

Jinx got Alice aside after a while and asked her bluntly when the wedding was to be, and who was to be the happy bride.

Alice bridled. "Oh, that nonsense!" she said.

"I thought he'd fallen in love with you both," he said.

"Oh, dear, no; that was all just a joke, that valentine. We understood that, Jinx. And you know, neither of us would want to get married. And having a husband around—goodness, look at Henrietta and all the trouble she has with that Charles!"

Later Jinx and Freddy and Mrs. Wiggins talked it over. It was very nice for Edward to have a comfortable home and be waited on hand and foot, but it was kind of hard on poor Uncle Wesley.

"I hate to see Emma and Alice acting so silly," Freddy said. "When really that Edward is just imposing on them."

"He's too fresh," said Mrs. Wiggins. "I can't abide a fresh duck."

"You said the other day you couldn't abide a bashful duck," Jinx said. "Make up your mind, cow."

"I can't stand either of 'em," Mrs. Wiggins

said. "This Edward seems to be two ducks, and I don't like either of them."

"How about roast duck?" said Jinx.

"My goodness, that gives me an idea!" Freddy said. "Look, do we really want to get rid of Edward?"

They agreed that they did. So that afternoon Freddy walked up into the woods and then swung around down to the duck pond as if he was coming from Witherspoons'. Alice and Emma and Edward were testing the water of the pond with their feet, undecided whether to go for the first swim of the season or not. Alice and Emma giggled and gave little quacking squeals, and Alice splashed water on Edward. "You're so brave, Edward," she said. "I know you're just pretending. You're just laughing at us poor timid girls!" Uncle Wesley sat gloomily on the bank with his back to them.

"Hi, Edward!" Freddy called. "Come here a minute. Look," he said in a low urgent voice. "I was just over at Witherspoons' and they were looking for you."

"Let 'em look," said Edward with a grin.

"O.K," said Freddy. "But from what they said, I think they know where you are. And there's something else they said too." He hesitated. "I hardly know how to tell you. But I must. It's Mrs. Witherspoon's birthday tomorrow, and—well, they're planning on roast duck for the birthday dinner."

Edward gave kind of a chattering quack, and staggered a little as he looked with consternation at the pig.

"They spoke of—of sage and onions," said Freddy sadly.

Edward stood perfectly still for a minute. Then he looked up suddenly at Freddy. "Say goodbye to everybody for me," he said, and then spread his wings and with a whoosh! was gone over the treetops.

"Gracious!" Emma exclaimed. "Where's Cousin Edward going? It's almost dinner time."

"Yes," Freddy said. "That's what I told him."

Chapter 12

The animals had a pretty uneventful trip south.
They were seen and followed once or twice by
hunters, but now that the snow was gone it was
easy enough to throw any pursuers off the track.
Jinx had decided to come along. He had got so
interested in painting that he hated to leave his
studio, but as he said, he had the rest of his life
to paint in, while a chance to have all sorts of
adventures in good company didn't come very

often. He ended by taking his paints along, packed with a double rule of molasses cookies Mrs. Bean had baked for them, and the rest of their baggage in the saddlebags attached to Jerry's saddle. Mrs. Bean had made the saddlebags out of an old blanket. Jerry was very proud of the saddle the prisoners at the jail had made for him, and wore it even when he went to bed.

Jinx didn't have any chance to paint on the road, for there was a lot to see and they traveled steadily. They sang a good deal—the old marching song that the Bean animals had sung on the trip to Florida, and the Boomschmidt marching song, and the campaign song Freddy had written when Mrs. Wiggins had been a candidate for the presidency of the First Animal Republic. Freddy didn't have time to compose new songs, but he did make up some verses to the tune of Froggy Went a-Courting. They were about Edward, and they went like this:

Edward went a-Courting, he did waddle,
   h'm—h'm.
Edward went a'courting, he did waddle
Through the brook and over the puddle,
   h'm—h'm; quack—quack.

He came to Lady Alice's hall, h'm—h'm.
He came to Lady Emma's hall
And his feet were so cold he could hardly
*   crawl, h'm—h'm; quack—quack.*

He took Lady Alice on his knee, h'm—h'm.
He took Lady Emma on his other knee,
And he said: "Will the both of you marry
*   me?" quack—quack; quack—quack.*

Lady Alice giggled and shook her head, tee—
*   hee.*
Lady Emma tittered, and they both said:
"We'll ask Uncle Wesley if we can wed,"
*   tee—hee; quack—quack.*

Uncle Wesley came and he said: "No, no!"
*   h'm—h'm.*
Uncle Wesley growled and he said: "No,
*   no!"*
But they pushed Uncle Wesley out in the
*   snow, quack—quack; no—no.*

Where shall the wedding supper be?
*   h'm—h'm.*
Where shall the wedding supper be?
Down in the barnyard under the tree, h'm
*   —h'm; h'm—h'm.*

The first that came was Jinx, the cat,
meouw—meouw.
The first that came was Jinx the cat,
He wore high boots and a big plug hat,
h'm—h'm; meouw—meouw.

The next that came was Leo, the lion,
woof—woof.
The next that came was Leo, the lion,
With his claws manicured and his mane
a-flyin', h'm—h'm; woof—woof.

The next that came was the rhinocer-us,
umph—umph.
The next that came was the rhinocer-us,
And he ate so much that he almost bust,
h'm—h'm; umph—umph.

The next that came was Freddy, the pig,
oink—oink.
The next that came was Freddy, the pig,
And with the bridegroom danced a jig,
oink—oink; quack—quack.

The last that came was old Witherspoon,
O dear!
With an axe in his hand came old Wither-
spoon

And chopped off his head by the light of the
moon, O dear! h'm—h'm.

And that was the end of the bashful duck,
h'm—h'm.
And that was the end of the bashful duck;
To end on a platter was just his luck, quack
—quack; h'm—h'm.

This made a good song, because they could
change it every time they sang it and make up
new verses. Even Jerry made up one, and it
wasn't a bad one either, about the next that
came being the rhino, Jerry, whose home was
on the wide, wide prairie. And when one of
them had made a new verse, they'd all sing it as
a quartet. Freddy carried the air, and Jinx sang
a kind of wailing tenor, and Leo sang bass, and
I don't know what you'd call what Jerry did. He
had a grunt that was as deep as a bull fiddle, and
when he hit the right note it sounded real nice.

It grew warmer as they traveled southward,
and pretty soon they met the spring, which was
traveling northward, and the grass was green
and the trees in bud, and there was arbutus in
the woods and thousands of birds, traveling up
with the spring. They would have liked to ask

the birds for news of any of the other circus animals that they might have seen, but the birds were much too anxious to get home and start repairing the damage that winter storms had done to their old nests to bother answering questions.

Early that afternoon they came down through some pine woods on to a hillside overlooking a wide, shallow valley. Down in the valley a racetrack was laid out, at one side of which was a grandstand, and flags were flying from the grandstand, into which crowds of people were pouring. Blanketed horses were being led around in an enclosure near the track and it was plain that there was going to be a race.

Everybody likes to see a race, so when Jinx suggested that they sneak down along the fence and get up close to the track on the east side where there was a little clump of trees, they started down. There was so much going on around the track that they reached the trees without attracting attention, and while they were waiting for the race to begin they decided to have lunch. Freddy had just started on his second cookie when a creaky voice said: "Y'all got anything to eat?"

The heads of the four animals jerked up as

if they had been pulled by a string, and they saw a large buzzard sitting on a limb above them. His plumage was as rusty as his voice, and one round greedy eye was fixed on the open cookie box.

"Thank you, yes; we have plenty," said Freddy with a grin.

"I ain't askin' if y'all got enough," said the buzzard. "I'm askin', could you spare a bite?"

"Oh, go away," said Jinx. "We haven't got anything you'd like anyway; we know what buzzards eat—just garbage."

"We prefer to call it left-overs," said the buzzard, looking reproachfully at the cat. "Buzzards, mister," he went on, "just clean up after untidy folks, like it might be you all, leavin' crumbs and banana skins all over nice clean landscapes."

"Well, there won't be any left-overs here, or any garbage either," said Jinx, "so you might as well beat it."

"Wait a minute," said Freddy. "You—what's your name?"

"Phil," said the buzzard.

"Well, Phil, if you can help us, we'll give you one of our cookies. We're looking for some animals that used to be with a circus, and maybe you've seen some of them." And he explained about Mr. Boomschmidt's animals.

But Phil shook his head. "They sound like right pretty animals," he said, "but in these yere woods there's only coons and foxes and squirrels and a few deer and possums. Tell you what there is, though," he said; "there's a big old snake lives down in the swamp t'other side the racetrack. He's twenty, twenty-five feet long, I reckon, and he's kind of a curiosity around these parts. He's—"

"Well, clip my whiskers!" interrupted Leo. "I wonder if that's Willy. Remember Willy, Freddy—our boa constrictor? What color is he, Phil? How's he marked?"

"Mister," said the buzzard, "he can be pink with yellow stripes and a long green moustache for all I know or care. I don't go round measurin' no snakes."

"We'll have to go down there," said Jinx. "Well, Phil, here's your pay." And he tossed him a cookie.

Leo watched the buzzard as he smacked his beak over the cookie. "You must be from the south, Phil, from your talk."

"*From* the south! I ain't *from* the south,

Yankee; I'm *at* the south. Virginia's my home."

"Virginia!" Freddy exclaimed. "You mean we're in Virginia already?"

Phil assured them that they were, and a little questioning brought out the fact that they were within ten miles of Yare's Corners, which was just over the mountain from the Boomschmidt place. They were discussing whether to push on at once, or to watch a race or two first, when two of the track officials came riding in among the trees. They had caught sight of the animals through their field glasses, and had come over to investigate.

"Jumping Moses, a lion!" said one.

"What is this—a menagerie?" said the other, who was a thin, middle-aged man with a wisp of grey whisker on his chin.

The first one said: "A lion and a pig and a cat and a—well, what is it, Henry—that creature there with a saddle on?"

"Good afternoon, gentlemen," said Freddy politely. "May I present my friend? He's a rhinoceros. Jerry, this is—ah—"

"Major Hornby," said the first man, bowing. "And this is Mr. Bleech, Henry Bleech. Are you . . . I see this saddle on—on Jerry,—are you planning to enter the third race?"

"No," said Freddy. "No, we were just watching—"

"We ought to have him, Major," said Mr. Bleech eagerly. "He'd be a great drawing card, this rhin—whatever he is." He turned to Freddy. "There's a purse of two hundred dollars, and your Jerry here—he'd have a good chance to win. You see it's a free for all, the third race. All the other races are for horses, but the third is for any animal *except* horses. But we've only three entries—a cow, a ram, and a camel. Is your Jerry fast?"

"A camel?" said Freddy. "Where's he from?"

"Belongs to some crazy old fellow over beyond Yare's Corners that used to run a circus," said the Major. "See here, I don't suppose you've got the money for the entry fee. It would cost you ten dollars to enter Jerry in the race. But I'll gladly pay it out of my own pocket if—"

"We always pay our own way," said Freddy coldly. The slighting reference to Mr. Boomschmidt had made him angry. "Excuse me." He drew his friends aside and held a short consultation. Then he came back. "I think we'll pay twenty dollars and enter both Jerry and Leo."

"That lion?" said Mr. Bleech. "See here, Major, I don't know that I want to ride my cow in a race with a lion. Suppose the lion forgot it was a race, and decided it was a chase? Eh? Suppose—"

"You need not worry, sir," said Leo courteously. "I never chase cows. Personally it seems rather unsporting."

"Leo will have to run without a rider," said Freddy. "Jinx will ride Jerry, because there'll have to be somebody to steer him, but nobody could ride a lion bareback. Is that all right?"

Major Hornby said it was and they all started down to the paddock. On the way, Freddy fished in the saddlebags and brought out a twenty dollar bill, which he handed to the Major. He didn't like the way Mr. Bleech eyed him when he was doing this, and when he had a chance he whispered to his friends that they'd better leave the saddlebags on during the race. A few extra pounds would make no difference to Jerry, and their money would be safe.

The Major explained that this free for all race was a very popular feature of the local race meets, and many people who didn't care much about horse racing would come for miles to see Mr. Bleech's cow, Galloping Nellie, run against Stonewall Jackson, the Major's racing ram, who were pretty evenly matched. Many more had come this time because of the camel. "And I wish we'd known beforehand that we'd have a lion and a rhinoceros," said the Major, "so we could have advertised everywhere. Why I daresay there are people who would come fifty miles to see a race like that."

So great, indeed, was the interest in the new entries, that most of the spectators crowded down into the paddock, and the first two races were run with only a handful of onlookers in the grandstand. The camel was in the paddock, too. He was a supercilious, ill-natured beast named Mohammed. When he saw Leo and Jerry, he gave a start of surprise, then turned his head away. But Bill Wonks, who was leading him, shouted and waved, and started to push through the crowd towards his old friends, when the third race was announced. "See you later," Bill called, then whacked Mohammed on the shins to make him kneel, so that he could get on his back.

The crowd dashed for their seats, and as Jinx leaped into the saddle and Jerry and Leo filed out after the camel on to the track, Freddy joined Major Hornby in his box in the front of the grandstand. Through the Major's field glasses he looked at the contestants as they lined up at the start.

"That's my son, Forrest, on Stonewall," said the Major, pointing to a boy of ten or eleven who was mounted on the ram. "Broke and trained Stonewall himself, and don't think that ram can't run. Trouble is, he hasn't any sense of direction—he ran the whole race in the wrong direction around the track last fall. He and Nellie met at the finish line, but Stonewall crossed it first. Of course the judges decided for Nellie, because she'd gone the right way. Didn't seem quite fair to me. It's the same distance either way."

"That's Jerry's trouble too," said Freddy. "No sense of direction. Or rather, he thinks there's only one direction—straight ahead. Only way we could figure out to steer him was to hold something out on a stick in front of his nose, and turn it whichever way you want to go. That's why Jinx has got that stick."

This was something Jinx and Freddy had figured out before the race. They knew that as soon as Jerry started to run he would shut his eyes and dash off in a straight line, which isn't much good on a circular track. But he had a keen sense of smell, and could follow a cookie dangled on a string in front of his nose. At least they thought he could, and Jerry agreed with them.

"I'm backing Stonewall to win, of course," said the Major. "Which one do you fancy, Mr.—ah—"

"Just call me Freddy," said the pig. "Well, I only know about my own entries, but I'd back Jerry. Lions get off to a quick start, but they sort of slow down after a minute, while a rhinoceros keeps building up his speed the longer he runs."

"What do you think of the camel?"

"He can run to beat the band," said Freddy. "But camels are contrary. Nothing makes them happier than disappointing somebody. If this camel thought his rider wanted to lose the race, he'd tear in ahead of everybody. My guess is, he'll come in last."

"You seem to know a lot about racing," said the Major, looking at Freddy with respect.

"I know a lot about animals, probably because I'm one myself. Oh, there goes the gun!"

There was a bang from the starter's pistol, and the animals were off. Leo took the lead, but the others came up quickly on either side and passed him. Freddy hadn't thought much of Galloping

Nellie. Cows aren't built for speed, and don't usually care much for it. But this cow was lean and rangy, and she stretched out her neck and held her tail straight up in the air, and with Mr. Bleech crouched on her back, skimmed over the ground like a racehorse. She had the inside position, next the rail, and at the quarter she was well out ahead. "Golly!" Freddy said to himself. "I wish Mrs. Wiggins could see this!"

It was a pretty exciting race. The people in the grandstand went wild. They stood on the seats and yelled and waved their hats and pounded one another on the back, and several people fell off their benches and got bruised, but they got right up again and didn't even feel it. The Major screamed: "Come on, Stonewall!" until he turned purple and lost his voice, but he kept right on opening his mouth, though no sound came out. At the halfway post, Nellie was still ahead. On her right the camel was swinging along at a smooth trot, but obviously not half trying, in spite of the way Bill was whacking her with his stick, while on his right Stonewall was coming up fast. Leo had dropped back and wasn't trying any more either. He was shaking his mane self-consciously, and Freddy knew that he was thinking that if he couldn't win, he could at least be admired for his good looks. On the outside, Jerry was only a little ahead of Leo, but he was beginning to pick up more speed, and Freddy was pleased to see that he was following the cookie very exactly. At the turns, Jinx would swing the cookie a little to the left, and Jerry would follow around the curve as smoothly as if he was running on rails.

Gradually Stonewall and Jerry began to catch up with Nellie. When they came into the stretch, the three were running almost neck and neck. The crowd screamed and yelled louder than ever, and several people fell right out of the stand. An elderly uncle of the Major's had his hat smashed down over his eyes so tight that he couldn't pull it off without help, and as nobody would help him, he never saw the last part of the race at all. Mr. Bleech was sitting far forward on the cow's neck and whacking her with the whip as if he was beating a carpet in the effort to maintain his lead, which was now less than a foot. But both Stonewall and Jerry came up and forged ahead and bore down side by side on the finish line.

Freddy was up on his chair now, yelling like the rest of them. "Jerry! Come on!" Of course Jerry couldn't hear him. But he came on just

He charged full tilt into the judges' stand.

the same. He came on like a steam engine, snorting with every bound, and the horn on his nose crept up past the heavy curved ram's horns, hung there a minute, and, fifty yards from the finish line, went on ahead.

And then it happened. A cookie hasn't any waist to tie a string around, and so when Jinx had fixed up Jerry's steering gear, he had punched a hole in the cookie and tied the string through the hole. But the string had gradually sawed through the cookie, which all at once broke in two and dropped to the ground. Suddenly the spicy cookie smell, which Jerry had been following, wasn't there any more. He swerved and brushed against Stonewall, and although he didn't hit him hard, the ram shot sideways through the fence as if he had been side-swiped by an interstate bus. In doing this, Stonewall clipped Nellie, who turned a complete somersault. Mr. Bleech flew in the air and landed flat on his face, just as Nellie came down and landed in a sitting position on top of him, so that their positions were exactly reversed. And Jinx gave a yell and jumped off.

And then Jerry swung still more to the left and instead of crossing the finish line he charged full tilt into the judges' stand, which was built up close to the side of the track. There was a terrific crash as the stand seemed to explode, and the air was full of planks and shingles and judges and pieces of two-by-four. And when the dust settled, the people in the stand saw the judges sitting, very grimy and confused, on the heap of rubbish that had been the stand, while the rhinoceros charged on across the turf inside the track, smacked through the fence on the other side, and disappeared among the trees.

Chapter 13

The judges, of course, had not really seen the end of the race, so when they had got up and brushed each other off, and felt each other over for broken bones, they went across and talked to the Major, who told them that it was the camel who had really won. For he had been the first to cross the finish line. So Bill Wonks got the purse of two hundred dollars to take home to Mr. Boomschmidt. Freddy went down to say hello to Bill and congratulate him.

"Well," said Bill, "the chief can use the

money all right. No thanks to this Mohammed though. Only reason we won was because there was nobody behind us but Leo, and Mohammed didn't know that or he'd probably have stopped and sat down. What you doing down here, Freddy?"

"Came down on business. I've got good news for you. How's Mr. Boomschmidt and everybody, and why didn't he come to see the race?"

"You know how proud he is," said Bill. "He won't go anywhere unless he's all shined up and his suit pressed. And he hasn't even a suit to press now—worn his clothes all out, and no money to buy new ones."

"We're going to change all that," Freddy said.

"I hope so. When I left this morning his mother was making a suit for him out of some old burlap bags. He just literally has nothing to wear, Freddy. Hey, here's Leo!"

"Well, scrub my toenails, Bill Wonks!" exclaimed the lion, holding out his paw. "How are you, Bill?" But without waiting for Bill's reply he turned to Freddy. "Say, that Mr. Bleech has ridden off after Jerry. At least he left his cow in a stall and got on his horse and rode in that direction. Hadn't we ought to keep an eye on him? Jerry's got all that money in the saddlebags."

"As long as the saddlebags are on Jerry, it'll take somebody bigger than that Bleech man to get the money out of them," Freddy said. "But we'd better get Jerry anyway. He's probably lying down and resting. He usually gets a head-ache when he runs into things."

"I don't believe that stand would bother him," said Leo. "It wasn't very solidly construc-ted. Concrete, now—that's what gives Jerry headaches."

Bill and the camel went along with them. They picked up Jinx in a patch of weeds behind the ex-grandstand. He too, had seen Mr. Bleech ride by on the trail of Jerry, but hadn't felt worried. And indeed when they got to the trees there seemed no cause for alarm. For Jerry was sleeping peacefully and the saddlebags were un-disturbed.

After a minute the rhinoceros opened his eyes. "Hello, Freddy," he said. "Did you get your bandage?"

"My what?" said Freddy.

"That bandage you sent for. To do up Jinx's paw. Mr. Bleech came for it. I said I didn't re-member your packing any bandage, but he said you told him it was in the saddlebags, so I let him look. He found it all right."

"Well, yank out all my incisors!" said Leo slowly. They all looked at one another in dismay, and then fell upon the saddlebags and pulled everything out. But the money was gone.

When Jerry got it through his head what a lowdown trick had been played on him, he was pretty mad. His little eyes got quite red, and he stumped up and down on his short legs, thinking of all the things he would do to Mr. Bleech when he found him.

"Which we probably won't," said Freddy hopelessly. "But we might as well try."

The buzzard was sitting in the tree above them with his greedy eyes glued to the cookie box, which was lying on the ground with the rest of the saddlebags' contents. Freddy took out a cookie and held it up. "Tell me where Henry Bleech lives and I'll give you this."

"Turn left at the gas station two miles down the Yare's Corners road," said Phil. "It's the third house on the right."

Freddy tossed him the cookie. Then he got up and repacked the saddlebags. "Come on," he said. "We'll go call on Mr. Bleech."

They made a detour around the racetrack, where amid a good deal of confusion another race was getting started. But Major Hornby saw them and came riding across to intercept them. Freddy went to meet him, and began apologizing for all the trouble they had caused. "And I hope your boy wasn't hurt when Stonewall went over the fence," he said.

"Not a bit. And as for the trouble—why you've given our little track a thousand dollars' worth of free advertising. The most sensational race we're ever likely to have."

"I hope the judges weren't hurt," Freddy said.

"They're tough," said the Major. "Anyway, nobody ever likes judges. Whatever decision they make, somebody's always mad about it. Even if they decide in your favor you never give them much credit. Everybody likes to see a judge bounced around a little."

Their road ran through the swamp where Phil claimed to have seen the big snake, and here Bill Wonks stopped and gave a peculiar whistle, and a minute later a huge boa came gliding out of the underbrush into the road. When he saw them he gave a delighted hiss. "Well, well, this is wonderful!" he said. He threw a couple of coils around Bill and hugged him so enthusiastically that Bill's eyes stuck out.

"Quit it, Willy!" Bill wheezed. "Don't be so darned affectionate."

"Can't help it," said the boa. "That's the way I feel. Why, I haven't seen a familiar face in months." But he uncoiled and went over to embrace Jerry.

The rhinoceros didn't mind being squeezed, but he seemed rather embarrassed by such a demonstrative greeting. "Hi, Willy," he grunted.

"You remember Freddy and Jinx," Bill said. "They've come down to get the circus started again." He stopped abruptly. "That is," he said slowly, "that's why they came, but—"

"Can't we just shake hands?" said Freddy, backing away from the advancing snake.

"We could if I had any hands," said Willy. "I'll just give you a little hug. How else can I show I'm glad to see you?"

"Well . . . all right," said Freddy. So Willy gave him a little hug, and then looked around. "Where's Jinx?'

But Jinx had gone up a tree.

"Jinx isn't very demonstrative," said Freddy, trying to get back the breath that Willy had squeezed out of him. "Why don't you hug Leo and Mohammed?"

Willy said he made it a rule never to hug any-body with claws more than three inches long. "And as for that moth-eaten, knock-kneed, bilious old grouch, Mohammed . . ." He stuck out his forked tongue at the camel, who made an ill-tempered, bubbling sound and kicked viciously at him.

"Come on," said Leo. "We're going to pay a call."

Mr. Bleech's house is kind of hard to describe. It was just a small white house, neither pretty nor ugly, neither large nor small, neither very well kept up nor badly run down. It was just a house. Jinx went in to reconnoiter while the others hid down the road. Presently he came back to report that somebody was moving around inside the house, but all the doors and windows were shut up tight. It was decided that someone should go to the front door and knock, and then if Mr. Bleech opened the door, Willy, who would be hiding down beside the little porch, would whip in and grab him. Leo and Bill both volunteered to do the knocking, but Freddy said no, it was his money that had been stolen; and so while Willy slid up into position from the side, the pig walked straight up the front path.

So Willy gave him a little hug.

But it didn't work out as they had planned it, for instead of coming to the door, Mr. Bleech threw up the window to the left of the porch, which was just above Willy, and the next thing the snake knew he was staring right down the barrels of a big double-barreled shotgun.

Freddy said afterwards that he never knew that a snake could glide backwards, but that's just what Willy did. He said: "Oh, excuse me; I guess I made a mistake," and he backed right down the path and out the gate. And when Mr. Bleech swung the gun towards Freddy and just said: "Git!" Freddy backed right after him.

When they got down to where their friends were hiding, Jerry was pacing up and down snorting, and madder than ever, and he said: "Look, Freddy, I'm going to handle this guy," and he went out into the road.

"No, no," said Freddy. "Come back. It's no use attacking him directly. We've got to use our heads."

"That's just what I'm going to use," said the rhinoceros. And he put his big ungainly head down so that the heavy horn on his nose almost touched the ground, and charged the house.

Well of course he had his eyes shut, and he

missed the house by about two feet. Bang! went one barrel of Mr. Bleech's gun, and then Bang! went the other barrel, but a rhinoceros has a hide two inches thick and I don't suppose the shot even tickled him. Out in back he hit a chicken coop, and he went on across a field in a cloud of feathers. He went quite a distance before it occurred to him to turn around and charge again from the other side.

"He's an awful poor shot," said Leo. "He needs somebody to aim him."

Mr. Bleech had slid two more cartridges into his gun, and as Jerry came thundering along he fired both barrels at once, but they had no effect. This time Jerry knocked apart a corncrib in the back, and he sheared off a sort of lean-to porch affair at the side of the house, but he still didn't get a direct hit.

"Well, he's whittling the guy's place down," said Leo. "But I'll aim him this time." So he stopped Jerry when he got to the road, and then he turned him around and pointed him and said: "Go!" And this time Jerry hit square between the two front windows. The bang of the gun was followed by a terrific crash and the tinkle of broken glass, and a yell from Mr.

Bleech. A cloud of dust puffed up and hid everything; evidently the Bleech house hadn't been dusted or swept in a good many years.

There were a few smaller crashes as Jerry went through a couple of partitions and a sideboard and a kitchen stove before he split the rear wall and got out into the open again.

But as the dust cleared they saw Mr. Bleech. He had stepped out into the yard and was waving a grimy handkerchief. Bill went out to stop Jerry, and Freddy and Leo went forward.

"Just for your information," Mr. Bleech drawled, "this house ain't mine: I rent it."

"I want my money," said Freddy. "Are you going to give it to me?"

"Money?" Mr. Bleech queried vaguely. "*Your* money?" He shook his head. "I ain't seen any money of yours, my friend."

"I see you don't intend to give it back," Freddy said. "So we will have to take other measures." Just what those measures would be, however, he had no idea. Mr. Bleech still had his gun, and they couldn't fight him. Even Jerry was no use, for out in the open it would be easy to dodge the rhinoceros's rushes. There was nothing to do but retreat.

Mr. Bleech stood fingering his wispy beard

as they turned and filed glumly out of the gate, and they heard him say, as if to himself: "Money? Whoever heard of a pig with money?"

Bill Wonks said: "That's the trouble, Freddy; if you go to the police, they'll never believe that a pig could have as much money as that."

"I could prove I had it," Freddy said. "Mr. Weezer counted it out to me."

"But you couldn't prove that this Bleech took it. It's just your word against his. And no judge will believe a pig's word against a man's."

"Sometimes," Freddy said bitterly, "I wish I'd never *been* a pig!"

"Well, you are one," said Leo, "so let's go on to Boomschmidt's."

But Freddy shook his head. "Oh, golly, Bill; I can't go there now. Why that money was the whole point of my coming down here. I guess— gee, I guess we'd just better go home again, Jinx."

"When you're right almost on his doorstep?" said Bill. "He'll feel terrible if you do that. Besides, he said if he won that two hundred at the races, he'd give us a big party, and he'd want you there."

"I haven't any heart for it," said Freddy gloomily.

"You don't have to be a partner in the circus, anyway," said Jinx.

"I'd rather leave the farm for ten years," said Freddy, "than to disappoint Mr. Boomschmidt like this."

The cat sniffed. "Very noble of you!" he said sarcastically. He really felt pretty badly about it himself, but cats don't like to show their feelings, and he expressed his disappointment and his anger at Mr. Bleech by picking on Freddy. Probably you can remember times when you've done the same thing yourself.

"I'm not noble at all!" Freddy snapped. "I'm just—" He broke off suddenly as a shadow swept across the road beside him, and he looked up to see the buzzard settling himself with a clumsy flapping of his big rusty wings on a bough overhead.

"Well, what do you want?" he said shortly. "We've got no more cookies for you."

"Y'all don't need to be so mean," said Phil. "I ain't askin' for anything. I got some right valuable information, if you want to trade."

Freddy looked at him a minute. Then he said: "Oh, give him a cookie, Jinx."

Phil gobbled the cookie, smacking his beak vulgarly over it; then he said: "That money of yours—it's in Mr. Bleech's right inside coat pocket. I was watching when he took it. I saw him put it there."

"There's a cookie wasted!" said Jinx disgustedly, and Freddy said: "Well, thanks for nothing. We could have guessed that. We could also guess that he will probably sleep with it under his pillow."

"He shore will," said Phil, wiping a few crumbs off his beak with a grimy claw. "And all you got to do is sneak in that hole in the side of the house after he's asleep—"

"Listen," said Freddy. "Hear that hammering? He's repairing that hole now. We can't sneak in through the side of a house. Or through locked doors and windows. No, we're licked, and we might as well admit it. Well, come on, animals. Let's go tell Mr. Boomschmidt and get it over."

Leo looked at the pig curiously. "I never knew you to give up so easily, Freddy," he said.

"I don't know that I've really given up," Freddy said. "But there's no use staying here now. Maybe Mr. Boomschmidt will have some idea about how to get it back."

"And in the meantime," said Jinx, "Bleech will have hidden it somewhere."

"No," said Freddy; "he'll keep it on him; it's the safest place for it. Gosh," he said, "I hate to tell Mr. Boomschmidt, though."

It was a pretty disappointed lot of animals that took the road to Yare's Corners.

Chapter 14

The animals' reception at the Boomschmidt farm was just as warm and just as sincere as if they had brought ten times the amount of money they had lost.

When he had heard their story, Mr. Boomschmidt laughed and said: "Why, good gracious, what are you all so downcast about, eh? Money! —what's money? It's—it's . . . Well, Leo, don't just stand there! Tell me what money is!"

"It's the root of all evil, chief," said the lion. "And boy, how you dig for it!"

"Why, I do not!" said Mr. Boomschmidt, looking embarrassed. "Well, maybe I do, but I don't really expect to find any." He turned to Freddy. "Leo's talking about the money that's supposed to be hidden in the house—the money the former owner, Col. Yancey, is supposed to have hidden before he went off to war and never came back eighty years ago. We've taken up a few floors and knocked holes in a few partitions looking for it. Places Madame Delphine told us to look when she was telling our fortunes. But we didn't really expect to find it. It's just something to do in the long winter evenings."

"Oh, yeah?" said Leo. "Well, it's funny you always acted so disappointed when there wasn't any money there."

"Why, of course we did! That's part of the game! And then too, Madame Delphine would be upset if we didn't act unhappy: you know she really believes it, Leo, when she tells your fortune."

"She told mine once," said Freddy, "and part of it came true. She told me I was going to have a stroke of luck soon, and sure enough, two days later I found a nickel."

"Well, my gracious, some of the things have to come true," said Mr. Boomschmidt. "She's told our fortunes hundreds and hundreds of evenings. She couldn't guess wrong about everything all the time."

Mr. Boomschmidt always sounded rather confused and sometimes sort of simple-minded, but he was really a very clever man. All this talk about the hidden treasure was really just to steer the conversation away from Freddy's loss, and to make him feel that though he had lost a large sum of money, Mr. Boomschmidt too had had almost the same kind of bad luck, in not finding Col. Yancey's hoard. It was pretty nice of him.

Indeed he only made one more reference to their loss. That was when Jerry tried to tell him how ashamed he was of being so stupid as to let Mr. Bleech open the saddlebags. He whacked the rhinoceros on the back. He had to whack pretty hard on Jerry's insensitive hide so that the rhinoceros would know he was being petted.

"Oh, forget it, Jerry," he said. "It's an ill wind that . . . oh, dear, I can't remember it! What is it that an ill wind does, Leo?"

"Blows nobody good, chief," said the lion.

"Blows nobody good?" said Mr. Boomschmidt. "That doesn't sound right. How can you blow *nobody* good? You can blow your nose good, and you can blow a horn good, but—"

"Skip it, chief," said Leo. "You're just mixing Jerry up. What you meant was that every cloud has a silver lining, wasn't it?"

"That's it—every cloud has a silver lining!" Mr. Boomschmidt exclaimed. "Now why didn't I say that in the first place?"

"Because you said something else," said Leo.

"Right," said Mr. Boomschmidt. "Well anyway, what I meant, Jerry, was: if this Bleech man hadn't stolen the money, we'd have had to do a lot of work. Getting the show organized and on the road, and all that. But now—well, we can sit back and enjoy ourselves. No work to do, nothing to worry about—I tell you, Jerry, I don't feel sorry a bit."

So Jerry felt better. Of course he wasn't very bright or he wouldn't have been taken in by such an argument. But all Mr. Boomschmidt wanted to do was keep him from being unhappy about it.

Mr. Boomschmidt gave them a party that night. They danced and sang songs, and Mr. Boomschmidt's mother baked them a big cake with "Welcome" on it in pink icing. Mrs. Boomschmidt was so happy that she cried nearly all the evening.

There wasn't any pigpen on the place, but

there was a lot of unoccupied barn space, because so many of the circus animals had left, and Freddy slept in a cage where Rajah, the tiger, had lived. He slept late, and when at last something disturbed him and he opened his eyes, it was to see Jinx and Leo and Willy standing in front of the cage and whispering and giggling.

When Jinx saw that Freddy was awake he nudged Leo, and then pretending not to know that the pig could hear him, he said: "My, my; what a ferocious animal! I certainly am glad that there are good strong iron bars between us. What did you say he was?"

"He's a wild African porkopotamus," said Leo. "Lives entirely on boiled mice and beet greens, with plenty of butter. Only one in captivity, and isn't that a break for everybody! Suppose there were a lot of them around."

"I think I've seen pictures of him somewhere," said Willy. "Only I don't remember that he was so homely."

"No," said Leo, "they've never been able to photograph him. They've tried, but when they point the camera and pull the trigger, the camera always blows up with a loud bang. Can't say I blame it."

"Ha!" said Freddy. "Very funny!" He got up.

"Stand aside!" he shouted. "The porkopotamus is coming out of his cage!" And he opened the door and rushed at them.

There was a sort of four-cornered tussle on the barn floor, which ended with Freddy held motionless in Willy's coils, while Jinx and Leo came up and sniffed doubtfully at him.

"Not very fresh," they agreed.

Then they all went up to breakfast.

On the way, Freddy said: "Willy, are you really thirty feet long? You don't look it."

"Don't know," said the boa. "Don't remember. But that's what it says on the sign I used to have on my cage."

So Freddy asked about it when they got up to the house. Mr. Boomschmidt said that how long anything was all depended on what kind of feet you measured with. And when Freddy said he supposed there was only one kind of foot, the one that had twelve inches in it, Mr. Boomschmidt said: "Oh, dear me, no! Look at my foot—about eight inches, wouldn't you say? And then look at Jinx's—about an inch. Do you remember what we used in measuring Willy, Leo?"

"We used my foot," said the lion. "Which is about six inches long. If you measured with a yardstick, you'd find Willy is about fifteen feet long."

Freddy started to say something more, but Leo shook his head at him. Later, the lion explained. "You'll embarrass the chief by asking questions like that," he said. "I suppose it's really cheating to advertise Willy as thirty feet long. But all circuses measure things that way. Willy's really the longest boa in captivity, but nobody'd believe it if we said he was fifteen feet and somebody else said theirs was thirty."

"Why don't you just advertise him as the longest boa in captivity, then?" said Freddy. "Then you wouldn't have to say things that aren't really true."

"Well, fry me in butter!" Leo exclaimed, looking admiringly at the pig. "That's an idea! My, that'll please the chief!"

After breakfast they all sat around on the porch and had a final cup of coffee, and Madame Delphine told their fortunes in the coffee grounds. Of course if Mrs. Boomschmidt had made the coffee in a percolator there wouldn't have been any grounds in the cups, but she was an old-fashioned cook who didn't hold, she said, with such new-fangled contraptions as percolators, and she just put the coffee right in with the water and some eggshells and stewed it up good. It was pretty strong for the smaller animals, but lions and rhinoceroses can drink anything. And I suppose Bill Wonks and Madame Delphine and Mr. Boomschmidt had got used to it. Anyway, when they had drunk the last drops and turned the cup upside down, there were plenty of grounds left sticking to the inside. And Madame Delphine would examine them and tell a fortune from them. It was a lot of fun, even when she had told the same person quite a different fortune the day before.

She told Jinx that she saw a crown and sceptre in his cup. "It is plain," she said, "that you come of a long line of very distinguished ancestors, and that royal blood flows in your veins. The crown is wrong side up, and that tells me that a base usurper now rules in your ancestral halls, but the sceptre is right side up, which means that you will, on some glorious day, not long hence, assume your rightful place on the throne of your forebears." Of course Jinx came of a long line of alley cats, and he knew it perfectly well, but he was pretty pleased all the same.

Then she saw a wedding ring and a needle in Bill Wonks' cup, and Bill blushed and fiddled with his moustache, for as everybody knew, Bill had for over a year been paying court to a lady in Yare's Corners, and the lady was a dressmaker.

Mr. Boomschmidt's cup had a house in it. The house had a very large chimney, and over the chimney was a dollar sign. At least that is what Madame Delphine said she saw, although it didn't look anything like that to Freddy, when he peered into the cup. But Madame Delphine seemed much pleased, and she said that at last they were getting closer to Col. Yancey's treasure, and she felt sure that if Mr. Boomschmidt would pull down the chimney . . .

"Why, dear me," said Mr. Boomschmidt excitedly, "that's the one spot we've never looked! The chimney! Of course! Best place in the house to hide anything. Just take a few bricks out and . . . Now why do you suppose we never thought of the chimney? Leo, how could we have forgotten to look there?"

"I guess it's because the house is built around the chimney, chief, and you'd have to pull the house down to get at it."

"You start monkeying with that chimney, boss," said Bill, "and I won't answer for the consequences."

"Oh," said Mr. Boomschmidt disappointedly,

"do you think . . . ? Well, maybe you're right, Bill. But I should think we could poke at it a little." He stopped then to listen to Madame Delphine, who was examining Freddy's cup.

Freddy, said Madame Delphine, could expect an important visit very soon. There the visitor was, right in the middle of the cup—that little sprinkling of grounds.

Freddy peered at it. "I don't recognize him," he said. "Looks sort of as if he'd been blown to pieces. Maybe somebody's going to send me a bomb."

Madame Delphine didn't like to have people try to be funny about her fortunes. I don't suppose she really believed in them herself, but she liked other people to—at least she liked them to pretend to. She handed the cup back to Freddy. "No use going on," she said, "if you take that attitude."

Freddy started to apologize, when Jinx said suddenly: "Hey, pig; there's your visitor right now." He pointed to the gatepost, out by the road, upon which Phil, the buzzard, was sitting, waving his ragged wings to attract Freddy's attention.

Freddy went down to the gate. "Hey, look," he said; "there isn't any use your following me

"There's only a few of those cookies left, and we want them ourselves."

around There's only a few of those cookies left, and we want them ourselves."

"Y'all are kind of hasty, ain't you?" said Phil. "If you think I'm after those cookies—well, I shore am. But I've got something to trade."

"Such as what?"

"Such as how to get into Bleech's house. I've been kind of projectin' around there, and I got a way figured out. But I want the rest of the cookies if I tell you." He smacked his beak in anticipation. "They shore are tasty! You suppose you could get me the recipe for 'em?"

"I probably could," said Freddy. "But what could you do with it?"

"I could look at it, after the cookies are gone. Be kind of like havin' a picture of your sweetheart to look at when she ain't there any more."

"Well, what's your scheme?" Freddy asked.

"Maybe you noticed the pipe from Bleech's kitchen stove," said Phil. "It don't go into the main chimney; it just goes up by itself through the roof. Now if you was to kind of ooze quietly up onto that roof tonight when the fire's been out for a while, and lift off the top section of pipe without being heard—"

"Oh, you're just wasting my time," Freddy interrupted. "Even Jinx is too big to go through a stovepipe, and he wouldn't do it anyway—get all ashes and soot, and he'd have to drop into the stove—"

"I wasn't figurin' on the cat," said Phil. "I was figurin' on that snake-friend of yours. Why it's easy! How come you didn't think of it yourself, I wonder?"

Freddy thought a minute. Maybe Willy could get down the pipe, after all. But if Bleech heard him, it would be—goodbye, Willy. . . . Still, if they were prepared to create some diversion outside—

Then he had an idea. "Wait here," he said, and went in and brought out the rest of the cookies. "That's all there are," he said, "but if this thing works out, I'll not only get you the recipe, I'll see that you get a whole fresh batch of them. Only I'd like you to stick around to-night; we may want your help. But don't say anything about this to the others, and specially to Mr. Boomschmidt. I'm working out a scheme, and everything depends on his not knowing about it till afterwards."

So Phil promised and Freddy went back to the porch.

"What did old rusty-tail want?" Leo asked.

"Oh, nothing," said Freddy. "Just chiseling

the rest of the cookies." And he changed the subject.

But later he spoke quietly to Jinx and Leo and Willy, and that night, after everybody had gone to bed, the four of them slipped out of the house and started off down the road to Yare's Corners.

Chapter 15

It was a clear moonless night, and they trudged along in silence—at least the three animals trudged; Willy, having no feet to trudge with, slithered. Willy was rather grumpy. He hadn't eaten anything since breakfast, in order to keep slim enough so he wouldn't get stuck in the stovepipe. Down the road they picked up Phil, who after a short conference flew on ahead to reconnoiter. Every house in Yare's Corners was dark except the doctor's, where a light burned in the office window; and Willy said: "I'm glad he's home. I hope he knowth how to treat gunthot woundth." Like all snakes, Willy had a tendency to lisp when excited.

"There aren't going to be any gunshot wounds," said Freddy firmly, and Jinx said: "Don't you worry, snake. We'll keep him occupied if he wakes up before you get in."

At Mr. Bleech's gate Phil was waiting, and reported everything quiet, and Mr. Bleech asleep and snoring in the upper front bedroom with all the doors locked and the windows nailed shut. The kitchen was a sort of lean-to affair attached to the back of the house, and the roof was low. Leo wasn't much of a climber, but by standing on his hind legs he got his forepaws over the edge, and then he dug his long claws in, and with Freddy and Willy boosting, got up on the roof without making too much noise. Then Willy followed, and Freddy and Jinx went around and crept up on the porch, to be ready to divert Mr. Bleech's attention from any suspicious sounds in the kitchen.

On the roof, Leo sat down and taking the stovepipe between his forepaws, lifted it quietly out. Now there was just a hole, which smelt of ashes and soot, but luckily no heat was coming up. Evidently Mr. Bleech had not yet repaired the damage that Jerry had done to his stove.

On the roof, Leo lifted the stovepipe out.

The two amateur burglars whispered together for a minute. Then Leo hooked his claws firmly into the shingles and braced himself, and Willy took two turns with his tail around the lion's body. "If I get stuck I'll give you two squeezes," he said, "and you pull me up." Leo nodded, and the snake started down the pipe.

Everything would have gone all right if Willy hadn't sneezed. But I guess you would have sneezed too if you had gone head first down a stovepipe into a firebox full of cold ashes. The first breath Willy took, the ashes went up his nose. It is really to his credit that he only sneezed once. But it was a good strong sneeze, even for a snake, and it blew one of the stove lids right off and sent it clattering to the floor.

Out on the porch Freddy and Jinx heard the racket. Mr. Bleech's gentle snoring stopped, there was a creak of bedsprings, and at once Freddy began pounding on the door.

As Freddy had hoped, the sound of the falling stove lid went right out of Mr. Bleech's mind when he heard the furious knocking. Convinced that whatever was wrong was at the front of the house, he grabbed his gun and started down the front stairs into the hall. "Shut up out there!" he shouted through the door. "Stop that racket!"

Freddy kept on pounding for a minute, to give Willy time to get out of the stove. Then he disguised his voice to a sort of whine and said: "Oh, excuse me, kind sir, but I am a little boy, and I am lost, and I want to find Yare's Corners. Would you please tell me which way to go?"

Now almost anybody would want to help a little boy who was lost in the middle of the night, but Mr. Bleech was a pretty mean man. Anyway, nobody in his senses would expect a kind action from a man who would steal from a rhinoceros. Mr. Bleech didn't open the door even a crack. "No, I won't!" he shouted. "And you get away from this house or I'll let you have a charge of birdshot. Now git!"

So Freddy pretended to burst into tears. He went down the front steps, and down the front walk, and as he went he cried and he howled and he bellowed so that you could have heard him a mile. I don't suppose any real boy could have made so much noise crying unless he was a giant or a concert singer. For a pig has piercing notes in his voice that very few boys can duplicate. But of course it was all to cover up any sounds that Willy might be making in the kitchen.

Mr. Bleech peered out through the keyhole,

for the performance really astonished him, but all he could see in the darkness was a small figure going down the path and out the gate. And when the bellowing had died away, he went back upstairs and got into bed again. And Freddy crept back and joined Jinx on the porch, where a few minutes later they were joined by Leo.

Nothing happened for a little while. And then there were faint grating sounds in the front door lock, and very slowly the front door opened and two or three feet of Willy came out. "Psst, Freddy!" he hissed. And when the pig had crept over to him, he whispered: "The money isn't under his pillow. I just looked. What do we do now?"

So Freddy gave the snake his instructions, and then Willy made a U turn and went back into the house.

There was some more quiet for a few minutes, and then a sudden yell, and thumpings, from upstairs, and the animals rushed in and up into Mr. Bleech's bedroom. Mr. Bleech was in bed, and it didn't look as if he was going to get out of it again in a hurry either, for the upper half of Willy was sitting on Mr. Bleech's chest, and the lower half of him was wrapped three times around both Mr. Bleech and the bed.

"Hi, Freddy," said the snake. "And what now?"

Freddy snapped on the electric light, and as he did so Mr. Bleech gave an exclamation of dismay. "You! Might have known it! Darned animals! You just wait! You'll be sorry for this to the last day of your lives."

Willy brought his tail forward and gave Mr. Bleech a slap on the side of the head that made his teeth rattle and left a long streak of soot on his cheek. Snakes are pretty muscular, and Willy only hit him gently because he didn't want to knock him unconscious.

"Take it easy, Willy," said Leo.

Freddy saw the shotgun standing in the corner by the bed. He got it and sat down in a chair. "Tell us where you've hidden the money," he said.

"I don't know anything about your old money," Mr. Bleech snarled.

"Give him a little squeeze, Willy," said Leo. "Don't squash him, just scrunch him a little."

So Willy scrunched him a little.

One scrunch was enough. When Mr. Bleech got his breath back he told them that the money was under a loose floor board in the closet. It was half a minute's work for Leo to claw up the board and bring the roll of bills out to Freddy.

"Seven dollars short," said the pig, when he had counted it. "Well, we won't grudge him that. I guess we've had seven dollars' worth of fun tonight. Come on, Willy."

Mr. Bleech didn't get up to see them to the door. He just lay there in his bed saying a lot of things that I wouldn't care to repeat, as they trooped out and down the stairs.

It was nearly one in the morning when they got back to Mr. Boomschmidt's, and they all sneaked off quietly to bed. But before Freddy went into his tiger cage he gave Phil the rest of the cookies. "And you stay around here," he said. "If everything works out right tomorrow morning, I'll write for that recipe, and as soon as it comes I'll get Mrs. Boomschmidt to bake you a double rule."

"Brother," said the delighted buzzard, "I ain't going to let you out of my sight." At least that was what Freddy thought he said, for Phil talked as usual with his mouth full, and it was hard to understand him.

Jinx and Freddy were up early next morning, and before breakfast Jinx saw Jerry and told him what had happened at Mr. Bleech's. Jerry felt a lot better when he knew that the money had been recovered, but he said reproachfully that they might have taken him along.

"We had to be very quiet, Jerry," said Jinx. "And—well, we were afraid maybe you'd get mad and bust up the house. If you'd have heard him yelling through the door at us, for instance—"

"I guess you're right, Freddy," Jerry said. "I get so *awful* mad, and then I have to do something. But my, I'm glad you got that money back!"

Then Freddy had a long talk with Madame Delphine, the result of which was that after breakfast, when they were sitting on the porch, Madame Delphine said: "I have a strange feeling that something very wonderful is going to happen today. What can it be?" she said, looking around distractedly. "Dear me, if I could only get a clue!"

"Maybe you could find out from the coffee grounds," Freddy suggested.

"Of course!" she said. "Let me see your cup." She looked at it and handed it back. "Nothing special there. Let's see yours, Bill."

She looked at several cups without finding anything significant, but when she came to Mr. Boomschmidt's she gave a loud dramatic cry.

"Ah! This is it! This *must* be. See here—the dollar sign as plain as the nose on your face! And below it . . . what is this?" She closed her eyes. "Let me think; let me think!" she muttered.

"Hush everybody," said Mr. Boomschmidt, leaning forward excitedly in his chair. "My gracious, stop rocking, mother! Willy, quit wiggling."

For several minutes Madame Delphine sat with closed eyes and her head cocked as if listening to distant voices. Then she began speaking, in a low thrilling voice which—Leo whispered to Freddy—used to cost the customers fifty cents extra when she was telling fortunes in her tent at the circus.

"I see," she said, "a dim room, a big room, with a sloping ceiling. I think it is an attic. I see a tall man. He wears a grey uniform and a grey slouch hat, and he has a sword at his side. In his hand he carries something. It might be a packet of letters. He takes it into a corner of the room; he kneels; he tucks the packet down into the corner where the roof meets the floor. Now I see him rise. He dusts off his hands. He—" She stopped suddenly, opened her eyes, and said in her natural voice: "Dear me, what are you all staring at? Did I tell you anything?"

"Come on!" shouted Mr. Boomschmidt, jumping to his feet. "Up to the attic. Let's see if we can find anything."

Animals and people, they all, with the exception of Jerry and Mohammed, rushed for the attic stairs. Even old Mrs. Boomschmidt picked up her skirts and ran; and the ancient house shook and trembled as they galloped up the long steep flights.

There was nothing much in the attic but some big trunks of circus costumes, and they shoved these aside and made for the corners.

"This seems the most likely corner, boss," said Leo, who had dropped back for a whispered word or two with Madame Delphine.

Mr. Boomschmidt knelt and fumbled around in the corner indicated, and sure enough, in a moment he rose with a shout of triumph, and in his hand a packet of twenty dollar bills. "We've found it!" he exclaimed. "Oh, glory me —look, boys and girls, here it is—Col. Yancey's money! O my gracious!" And he seized his mother about the waist and waltzed her around until the dust that her flying skirts raised from the attic floor set them all to sneezing.

Chapter 16

They clattered down the stairs, shouting and laughing, but when they got back to the porch Mr. Boomschmidt called for quiet. "There's just one thing," he said. "This money belonged to Col. Yancey. See?—it says on the paper: Property of Col. Jefferson Bird Yancey. Now Col. Yancey is dead, and I understand he left no living relatives. So who does this money really belong to? Does it really belong to us?"

"If the house belongs to you, the money you found in it belongs to you," said Jinx, and the others agreed.

"Yes," said Mr. Boomschmidt. "Yes, I suppose so. I just want to be sure."

"Never look a gift horse in the mouth, chief," said Leo.

"Horse?" Mr. Boomschmidt screwed up his face in puzzlement. "What are you getting at, Leo? There's no horse here. Lions, boas, pigs, cats—no horse. I'm afraid you're a little over excited, Leo; perhaps you'd better go in and lie down on the couch for a while."

"You know what I mean," said the lion. "I just mean, if you get a present, it isn't nice to ask many questions about it."

"A present?" said Mr. Boomschmidt, looking questioningly at Leo. "A present from whom?"

"Well," said Leo, looking embarrassed, "I guess it's a present from Col. Yancey, isn't it?"

"Oh," said Mr. Boomschmidt. "Oh, Col. Yancey. Yes." He began counting the money. "Fifteen hundred . . . sixteen hundred . . . seventeen hundred— Funny! It's almost exactly the same amount that—excuse me mentioning it, Freddy—but it's almost exactly what that man stole from you."

"Why—is it?" said Freddy nervously. "Yes, of course it is. Odd, eh?"

"Just a coincidence, chief," said Leo, trying to make up for his slip of a minute earlier.

"Life is full of coincidences like that," said Freddy. "I remember one time—"

"Excuse me, Freddy," said Mr. Boomschmidt, "but my gracious! we haven't time for reminiscences today. We've got to get organized. Got to get the tents and wagons out and look them over, got to get new crews together. . . . Bill, you have the addresses of most of the old employes, haven't you? Well, send 'em all telegrams: 'Come at once; circus reopening immediately.' Leo, you and I will see how many of the animals we can round up. Gracious, that's a big job! Got any ideas about it, Freddy?"

Freddy told him how he had found where Leo was, by showing the birds a picture of a lion.

"Splendid!" said Mr. Boomschmidt. "Isn't that a splendid idea, Leo? I knew we could count on you, Freddy. And by the way, how about coming in as my partner? The offer still stands. We need you; eh, Leo?"

"Sure do, chief."

Freddy shook his head. "A partner has to bring something to the partnership," he said. "I was to bring the money, and you, the know-how and equipment, remember? But I lost the money—"

"You raised it, didn't you?" said Mr. Boomschmidt. " 'Tisn't your fault you lost it. Now don't say no. You don't want to hurt my feelings, do you?"

Freddy said of course not.

"Well, my feelings hurt awful easy," said Mr. Boomschmidt. "You just ask Leo if they don't."

"That's right, Freddy," said the lion. "The chief's awful sensitive. Why, I've known him to cry half the night, just when one of the snakes forgot to come in and say goodnight to him. Heard him myself in his bedroom, sobbin' and moanin' and—"

"There, there; that's enough, Leo," said Mr. Boomschmidt. "No need to overdo it. Well, Freddy, what do you say?"

"I guess I ought to tell you," said the pig. "I didn't really want to be a partner in the show. Oh, I know it would be fun, and I'd enjoy being with you and all the animals, and on the road and everything. But it would keep me away from the farm all summer. And I wouldn't like that."

"I see," said Mr. Boomschmidt. "Yes, yes; should have thought of that myself. Well, that settles it, then. But I tell you what I'm going to do. I'm going to make you a sort of partner just the same. When Boomschmidt's Colossal and Umparalleled Circus goes on the road, it's going to be—not just Boomschmidt's, but Boomschmidt & Company's. And you're going to be the Company—or abbreviated: Co. Not that we'd want to abbreviate you, Freddy; on the contrary. Anyway, I wouldn't know how to abbreviate a pig, even if I wanted to."

And then as Freddy started to protest: "Now, now," he said. "What was it Leo said? Leo, what . . . Oh, I remember: mustn't look a gift horse in the mouth. Seem to be several gift horses prancing around here this morning. Well, let's keep their mouths shut, eh, Freddy?"

Freddy didn't say anything for a minute, but he thought: "I bet he knows! He knows that's my money."

Then he looked at his friend and smiled. "Well," he said, "I suppose one good gift deserves another."

"That's the ticket!" said Mr. Boomschmidt. "I couldn't have said it better myself. At least, I don't think I could. By the way, that reminds me of a queer thing." He pulled the big roll of bills out of his pocket. "You know, that Col.

Yancey, he hid these bills away back in the sixties. But I just happened to glance at this top one, and it says 'series of 1934.' Now that's a very funny thing. How do you account for it? Leo, what do you think?"

Freddy wasn't used to handling bills much, and it had never occurred to him that they would have dates on them. Of course Col. Yancey couldn't have hidden a nineteen-thirty-four bill back in the sixties. He said to himself: "So that's what made him guess where the money came from!"

Mr. Boomschmidt was glancing from Freddy to Leo, waiting for an answer. He had a very puzzled look on his face, but whether it was real, or just put on for the occasion, nobody could tell. You never could, with Mr. Boomschmidt.

Freddy couldn't think of a thing to say. But Leo said: "I expect those government printers —they were pretty careless in the old days—and they probably got a nine for an eight. Probably it was really the series of 1834."

It was a pretty weak explanation, but it seemed to satisfy Mr. Boomschmidt. He stuffed the bills back into his pocket, and Freddy was glad to see them disappear, for he had looked at the top bill too, and there were a number of things on it that couldn't possibly have been on a bill in 1860.

I don't suppose Freddy was any more unobservant than anybody else. The most interesting thing about a bill is its value, naturally; and so the only thing most people look at is the number: one or two or five or ten. I don't suppose you can tell offhand yourself whose picture is on the one dollar bill, or the five or ten either.

But although Freddy still wasn't sure whether or not Mr. Boomschmidt knew about the money, he didn't have time to worry about it. For Mr. Boomschmidt had got out his silk hat and put it on, and that meant that he was again a circus man; and he tore around the place, firing off orders like a machine gun, so that the plantation, which had been a quiet peaceful place when Freddy had got there, was turned into a regular factory, with people and animals running in all directions, and hammering, and sending telegrams, and overhauling gear, and doing the thousand things that had to be done to get the circus started again. Nobody even had time to think how funny the contrast was between Mr. Boomschmidt's silk hat and his burlap suit.

For three days Freddy and Jinx worked at a

big sign. It was a piece of canvas eight feet square, in the center of which were lettered these words:

BIRDS, ATTENTION!

A generous reward is offered for news of any of these animals. Have you seen any of them? Have you heard any unusual squeals, roars, squawks, howls or gibberings? If so, contact Mr. Boomschmidt at once. For any information you will be generously paid.

And then, all around the edge, they painted pictures of elephants, yaks, tigers, camels, zebras and all the other animals who had once been part of the circus. It wasn't as hard a job as it seems. Jinx would get some animal about half painted, and then he would ask Freddy what it looked like. Maybe Jinx had started to paint a tiger, but if it looked more like a camel, he would say so, and then Jinx would make his legs a little longer, and give him a hump, and take off the stripes. Lots of artists would have much better pictures if they would work by this method.

Bill Wonks nailed the sign to the roof of one of the barns, and it wasn't long before birds began dropping in with bits of information, a good deal of which was of value. Freddy posted Phil on the gable end of the barn, and he interviewed the visitors so intelligently that he was presently appointed Investigator in Charge of Bird Claims. On information received, he even made a number of trips, one of them as far as Tennessee, to bring in animals. By the end of the first week the circus had recovered four zebras, a gnu, a skunk, an aardvark, a family of monkeys and two alligators. The two elephants and the tiger who were living in the zoos in Washington and Louisville also came in.

The weather was getting warm now and one day Freddy, who had gone into Yare's Corners to get a box of cookies which Mrs. Bean had shipped him, was sitting in the shade by the side of the road, cooling off, when two boys came along. The sound of their voices woke Freddy up, and he heard one of them say: "I don't want zebras. But I'll trade you my elephant for two giraffes."

"Good gracious!" said Freddy to himself. He was still a little soggy with sleep, but he jumped up and ran out into the road.

"Excuse me," he said, "but did I hear you correctly? Did I hear one of you offer to trade two giraffes for an elephant?"

"Sure," said one of the boys. "He's got an elephant I want, but I don't see why I should have to give him *two* giraffes for him, do you? Giraffes are just as scarce as elephants."

"Listen," said Freddy. "There's a reward for both elephants and giraffes—didn't you know about it?"

"How much?" said one boy, and the other said: "Money?"

Freddy was still so sleepy that he couldn't think very clearly, and he hesitated. It would be worth quite a lot to Mr. Boomschmidt to get these animals back, but these boys probably didn't ever have much money. So he said: "A dollar apiece."

He had expected that they would want a good deal more than that, but to his surprise their mouths fell open and they both said: "Gee whiz!" They were so astonished that they said it without closing their mouths.

Freddy was rather astonished too, but he thought he'd better close the bargain before they thought better of it. "Lead me to them," he said, and fished three dollars out of his pocket.

But the boys didn't lead him anywhere. They dug in their own pockets and brought out handfuls of animal crackers.

Then Freddy's mouth fell open. "Oh, gosh!" he said, and he didn't close his mouth when he said it either.

"What's the matter?" they asked.

"Matter?" said Freddy, gasping a little. "Matter? Oh, nothing. Why, nothing at all." He wasn't going to let them know what a stupid mistake he had made. He held out the three dollars.

They sorted out the elephant and two giraffes and handed them to him in exchange for the money. And then Freddy did what I think was the only thing to do under the circumstances, and a pretty bright thing too. He put the two giraffes and the elephant in his mouth and chewed them and swallowed them, and then he smiled brightly and said: "Thank you very much. Good afternoon," and walked off. And he had the satisfaction—although perhaps it wasn't three dollars' worth—of seeing their mouths fall wider open than ever. And they stayed that way, too, as they stood and watched him until he was out of sight.

So more and more animals came, and the men who had worked for Mr. Boomschmidt before gave up the jobs they had found and came too, for they all liked to work for him; and the tents were got out and put in shape, and the wagons were painted, and then one day along towards the first of June, Mr. Boomschmidt, in a brand new suit of red and yellow checks and with his silk hat on the back of his head, rode out of the gate into the road. He touched his trick horse, Rod, on the shoulder, and Rod stood on his hind legs and Mr. Boomschmidt waved his hat three times around his head and shouted: "Forward!" And then he rode on up the road, and one by one the gaily painted wagons creaked out through the gate and followed him, and as they rode, the animals sang a song that Freddy had made up for them.

We're out on the winding road again,
The road where we belong;
By hill and valley, by meadow and stream,
On the road that's never too long.

Never too long is the winding road,
Though it climbs the steepest hill
Though dark the night, and heavy the load,
When the rain drives hard and chill.

For the stormiest weather will always
mend;
There's a top to the highest hill;

But the winding road has never an end,
  Whether for good or ill.

And we travel the road for the love of the
      road,
  For love of the open sky,
For love of the smell of fields fresh mowed,
  As we go tramping by.

For love of the little wandering breeze,
  And the thunder's deep bass song,
Which rattles the hills and shakes the trees
  Like the roar of a giant's gong.

For love of the sun, and love of the moon
  And love of the lonely stars;
And the treetoads' trill, and the blackbirds'
      tune,
  And the smell of Bill Wonks' cigars.

And there, where the road curves out of
      sight,
  Or surely, beyond that hill,
Adventure lies, and perhaps a fight,
  And perhaps a dragon to kill.

Or perhaps it's a brand new friend we'll
      make,
  Or a haunted house to visit,

Or a party with peach ice cream and cake,
  Or something else exquisite.

So now for us all, for pigs and men,
  For lions and tigers and bears,
The open road lies open again,
  And we toss aside our cares,

And we sing and holler and shout Hurray!
  No matter what the weather
For we'll not be back for many a day
  While we're out on the road together.

They had gone only a mile or two, however, when Freddy saw Phil sitting on a fence by the side of the road. Buzzards are never very tidy looking birds at any time, but Phil looked worse than usual, as he raised a shaky claw to salute Freddy. The pig went up to him.

"For goodness' sake, Phil," he said, "what ails you? You look terrible!"

Of course that's no way to greet anybody, even a buzzard who probably knows that he looks awful even when he feels all right. But Freddy was really quite shocked at the bird's appearance.

"I feel right awful, Freddy," the buzzard croaked.

"Want a cookie?" said Freddy. "We've got a couple in the—"

"Don't," moaned the buzzard despairingly. "I never want to see a—a—" He broke off. "I can't even name 'em. It makes me sick to even hear the word."

"Why, what's the matter?"

"Well," Phil said, "I reckon I sort of made a pig—oh, excuse me; I mean I made a hog . . ." He stopped and shook his head irritably. "You'll have to excuse my bad manners," he said apologetically. "I mean, I ate too many. I ate the whole double rule. I shore was sick! I like to have died; that's why I ain't been around this last month."

Freddy was too concerned over Phil's condition to be offended by the tactlessness of his remark about pigs. "You'd better see Mr. Boomschmidt," he said. "He'll know what to do for you; the circus animals are always eating too much of something or other, and he has to dose them for it."

Phil agreed listlessly, and Freddy ran up to the head of the line and got Mr. Boomschmidt.

Mr. Boomschmidt always carried a bottle of castor oil and a tablespoon in his pocket when he was on the road, for as Freddy had said, one or another of the animals was always overeating, and it was too much trouble to hunt around in the wagons for the medicine when it was needed several times a day. He gave Phil a good dose.

To their surprise Phil didn't try to get away, but opened his beak obediently, and even smacked it when the oil was all down.

"Right pleasant stuff," he said. "What is it?"

"Castor oil," said Mr. Boomschmidt.

"Never heard of it," said Phil. "Why, I feel better already."

"Good grief!" said Mr. Boomschmidt. "Where were you brought up?" Then he shoved his hat over to the back of his head and stared thoughtfully at the buzzard. "How'd you like to join our show?" he asked.

"Like it right well," said Phil. "But what good would I be in a show?"

"Well," said Mr. Boomschmidt, "there's a lot of tidying up to do around the grounds after the show's over. You could do that. But what I'd really like to have you for is to act as a good example to the other animals."

"Me?" said Phil. "A buzzard can only be a good example to another buzzard, and as there ain't any other—"

"Oh, my goodness," said Mr. Boomschmidt,

"let me do the talking, will you? See here; I have a lot of trouble getting my animals to take this oil. I can't imagine why, can you, Leo? Eh, can you imagine why? —Oh, Leo isn't here. Well, I'll answer myself then. No, I can't. Oh dear, now where was I? —Oh yes; oil. Well, you see, when one of 'em objects, then I can get you and give you some and show 'em how good you are about taking it, and then they'll take it without any fuss. We won't tell 'em you really like it. You can make faces—or maybe you don't need to; your face . . . h'm. But you do like it, don't you?"

"Try me," said Phil.

So Mr. Boomschmidt gave him some more, and Phil smacked his beak again.

That was how Phil joined the circus.

So the show went on north, stopping at the larger towns to give performances, and at last they reached Centerboro. It has often been said that Mr. Boomschmidt gave the finest performance of his career there. But this has been written about so many times that I will not repeat here what everybody already knows. For those who wish to refresh their memory of this great event, however, I recommend the account published in Freddy's newspaper, the Bean Home

He gave Phil a good dose.

News, of that date. It is complete, well considered, and—I think—not too fulsome.

Mr. and Mrs. Bean were in a box right down close to the ring, and all the farm animals were with them. They clapped and cheered with the rest. But the act that really made the whole audience whistle and stamp until the big tent bulged out like a paper bag that you blow up, was the one that Freddy put on. He rounded up the mice who had been living in the barn he had rented, and he had them hide all around the edges of the tent and among the seats. Then a bugle blew, and Mr. Boomschmidt announced that the famous Pied Piper of Centerboro had been engaged at great expense to put on his unique and stupendous mouse-charming act. Then Freddy marched out in his Pied Piper suit, blowing the first seven notes of Yankee Doodle on his fife, and out from all sides the mice came scampering, and they lined up behind Freddy, and he marched them three times around the ring and then out to the dressing rooms.

It was a great success. Of course several ladies fainted away and had to be carried out and revived with smelling salts, but as Bill Wonks said,

"A circus act ain't really a success unless a few people get so scared they keel over."

Indeed so great a success was it that Freddy stayed with the show nearly all summer, and gave his performance in most of the big towns of the eastern seaboard. For as long as he wasn't a real partner, and really didn't have to stay with the show, he didn't mind. You see, he had accomplished what he had set out to do. Just as he had managed to get his path cleared of snow without having to do any shoveling himself, just so he had managed to raise the money and get it into Mr. Boomschmidt's hands, without having to become a partner.

But one funny thing happened along in August. They had swung around through the southern part of New York State, and stopped to give a show in Tallmanville. Freddy and Leo didn't join the parade through the town before the show. But they took their regular part in the performance, because they didn't think that Mrs. Guffin cared for entertainments. Leo said she never went to anything.

But she came. She came along with the people who looked at the menagerie before the performance, and when she saw Leo she recognized him. She was pretty mad. She made quite a fuss in front of the cage. She told all the people around her what had happened in the spring, and of course her account of it wasn't much like the truth, and some of the people got mad too and advised her to call a policeman. But she said no, she was going to do better than that. She was going to wait till Leo was doing his balancing act in the ring, and then she was going to get right up in her seat and denounce him, and Mr. Boomschmidt, who had probably stolen him from her. And then she would call the police.

Leo sent for Freddy.

"I don't know what she can prove," said the pig. "But I suppose she can make it unpleasant for us."

"Well," said Leo, "no use worrying the chief with it. He can't do anything. We'll just have to go on with the show."

"Nothing else to do," said Freddy. "I never thought she'd come around."

Freddy's act came just before Leo's, and when he marched in, sure enough, there was Mrs. Guffin right down in front, and looking mad enough to chew carpets. Luckily she didn't see beneath the Piper's suit to the pig underneath.

And then when he started to blow Yankee

Doodle—which by this time he had learned, all but the last half—the funny thing happened. For the ferocious Mrs. Guffin was afraid of just one thing on earth: she was afraid of mice. And when they came tumbling out from under the seats she gave a loud yell and fell over in a dead faint. It took four strong men to carry her out of the tent, and by the time she had come to enough to be mad again, the show was over.

"Well, curl my eyelashes!" said Leo. "I wish we'd known she was scared of mice when we were here before. We'd have had a lot easier time with her."

"Oh, I suppose so," said Freddy. "But it wouldn't be as much fun to look back on. You know, if we knew everything beforehand, things wouldn't be much fun, would they?"

That was really one of the smartest things Freddy ever said.

A NOTE ON THE TYPE

The text of this book was set on the Linotype in Baskerville. Linotype Baskerville is a facsimile cutting from type cast from the original matrices of a face designed by John Baskerville. The original face was the forerunner of the "modern" group of type faces.

John Baskerville (1706-75), of Birmingham, England, a writing-master, with a special renown for cutting inscriptions in stone, began experimenting about 1750 with punch-cutting and making typographical material. It was not until 1757 that he published his first work. His types, at first criticized, in time were recognized as both distinct and elegant, and his types as well as his printing were greatly admired.